INTERSTELL᾽
PROG

YOUR mate is out there. Take the test today and discover your perfect match. Are you ready for a sexy alien mate (or two)?

VOLUNTEER NOW!

interstellarbridesprogram.com

1

*A*tlan Warlord Jorik, Interstellar Brides Processing Center, Florida, Earth

MY BEAST HAD STIRRED at the sight of her walking past the gated entry to the Interstellar Brides Processing Center. With her curvy body swaying seductively, a human guard had stared intently, obviously enjoying the sassy sway of her rounded hips and the jiggle of her large breasts. She wore what the humans called shorts, which showed off long, shapely legs and too much soft skin. Her hair fell halfway down her spine, a shimmering pool of liquid black. So straight. So dark the light flashed in odd shades of the deepest blue when the sunlight hit it just right.

Next to me, Sergeant Derik Gatski, a brute of a man—for a human—whistled under his breath, but I heard him. Loud and clear. "How about some fries with that shake?"

Before he'd finished the sentence, I had his neck in my hand, his feet dangling beneath him. "You will not disrespect that female. Ever."

His blue eyes widened in fear as he stared at me but knew better than to reach for the ion blaster strapped to his hip. Wisely, he held his hands up in the air, palms out. "My apologies, Warlord, I didn't realize she was yours."

I didn't correct him—she was not mine...yet—but I did settle him back onto his feet without crushing the fragile windpipe beneath my palm. His grin was annoying, but I turned away from the knowing look in his eyes and craned my neck for one last view of my future mate.

She was going to be mine. I'd been courting her for weeks, going as often as I could to her ice cream store to speak to her. The first time she'd seen me, she'd been shocked. Afraid. Of my size. My deep voice. My strength. Of me.

That was not what I needed. I needed her hot and willing, her soft body pressed to mine, my cock buried deep, her cries of pleasure driving my beast wild.

I didn't want her to fear me. I hoped for more. I was nearly ready to press my claim. My beast was more than eager, angry that I was taking so damn long to ease his need.

But I was not out of control, not yet. I did not suffer from Mating Fever. I still had a choice. And I chose her.

Mine.

My beast growled the single word inside my mind as she hurried across the street, avoiding the protestors marching on the other end of the building. Her haste, no doubt, because she would be late for her clock. She'd said something about clocking in once, but I didn't understand why she would wish to be inside a clock. Antiquated human technology, clocks. And most were far from accurate.

I had no idea what my female was referring to half of the time we talked, but I liked what I saw. What I heard. Everything about her. Not liked. That was a weak word. An Earth word. I craved. My cock lengthened and my balls ached to fill her. My palms itched to grip those wide hips and make her mine.

Oh yes, mine.

I wanted the fries *and* the shake.

My beast agreed. The primitive side of me had awakened the first day I saw her, not because of her delectable curves, but because of her scent. Each day when she walked past on her way to work, we caught her unique sweetness in the air. Cookies and vanilla. I knew of neither of those Earth things before my arrival here a few months ago, but my beast really liked them. In our visits to her store, man and beast had become addicted to the taste of both. My mouth watered, wondering if she'd be as sweet tasting as her ice cream... everywhere.

At ten each morning, she walked past, her T-shirt—which didn't hide the full swells of her breasts—had the words Sweet Treats written across the back. I had since learned Sweet Treats Ice Cream Shop was a frozen dessert store a few blocks from the processing center, but I preferred to think the words on her clothing referred to her specifically. I wanted her to be my sweet treat.

I wanted to hear her say my name. I ached for her.

I'd been stationed on Earth for four months now. While we were allowed to leave the compound, we were also given a perimeter of five miles in which to travel. The presence of alien guards working at the Bride Processing Center was well-known, but we were only familiar to those who lived and worked nearby. If we ventured too far, Earth's governments believed the presence of seven-foot, gold and bronze Prillon giants, or an eight-foot Atlan in his beast form might cause a public panic. The human government had grudgingly allowed alien guards to man the perimeters of the seven processing centers on Earth. Brides and soldiers came through these doors, and we needed both. After the humans had proven themselves incapable of keeping spies and traitors out of the centers, Prime Nial had demanded better security.

Earth's governments had reluctantly agreed, but demanded we work with the humans. Hence the male guard who had dared disrespect my female, and the human female behind him. The two Earth soldiers were my constant companions when I was on guard duty, my human liaisons.

Keepers, more like, to keep the big bad Atlan from turning into a monster and eating babies.

Duty held me at the processing center

for another two hours, and I spent every single minute thinking of her. Not the paranoid humans who paced on the sidewalk across the street while holding strangely worded signs. I'd given up attempting to make sense of their words long ago. Slogans such as *'E.T. Go Home!'*, *'Aliens are STEALING our women!'*—the addition of the larger letters a source of many jokes within the guards' quarters each day—and *'Your daughter should not be an alien sex slave.'*

Sex slave?

I thought of the female I wanted to make my own and cringed. Humanity had a lot to learn. Our females were revered. Respected. Treated with the utmost care and treasured for what they truly were... precious.

We did not torture or kill them in fits of rage or jealousy. We did not take their bodies without permission, beat them or shame them. Any child was valued, regardless of who the father had been. The sign-carrying humans accused us—the Coalition worlds—of being savages.

Based on what I'd seen on this world's news and entertainment screens, every single woman on planet Earth would be better off somewhere else.

Maybe we should take all the females and let the Hive take the rest of them.

My beast growled in agreement, ready to emerge and beat every single one of those idiot humans senseless. More often than not these days, my beast had just one word running on repeat in my mind. *Mine. Mine. Mine.*

"Hey, Jorik. You with me?" The human guard who'd grinned at me two hours ago slapped me on the arm to get my attention. "Jorik? We've got incoming."

I stood in silence, waiting for the human male who reeked of alcohol and tobacco smoke to come closer.

"Looks like he's high. Can't even walk." Derik took a step forward, his small body more annoyance than effective deterrent should I choose to throw the human off the grounds. Still, I was content to allow Derik to deal with this problematic member of his own species. "Let me handle him. This guy's stoned out of his mind. Don't go beast on him, Jor—"

I fucking hated that nickname.

Behind the would-be intruder, Warden Morda walked toward the security gate for her shift, badge in hand—a hand that was shaking so badly she attempted to scan her card three times without success.

Was the quiet female so terrified of the smelly human that she could barely function? If she was this nervous, here, where the guards were ready to protect and defend her, how afraid was she elsewhere?

Enough of this.

I walked to the gate, gently removed the badge from Warden Morda's hand and scanned her through myself, holding the gate open for her and using my large frame to block her view of the drunken idiot currently in a screaming match with Derik.

The warden glanced up at me, then quickly away, as always. She was nothing like Warden Egara. Where Egara was fierce and fearless, this small female seemed to be frightened of her own shadow. She barely spoke and would not often look at the warriors who would gladly lay down their lives to protect her. She was a Warden of the Interstellar Brides Program. She gave hope to warriors fighting across the entire galaxy that they may be matched.

"Greetings, Warden Morda. Do not allow this foolish drunkard to frighten you. I would never allow him to hurt you."

She jumped, as if I'd startled her with an act of common courtesy. "Thank you, Warlord Jorik." She smiled shyly and hurried inside.

Strange female, that one. And her scent was heavy with some sort of cloying flower I did not find pleasant in the least. But she was important to the warriors in the Coalition Fleet, to Earth's protection, to many lives. She was small, fragile and female. That was all I needed to know to offer her my protection.

Once Derik chased away the idiot, our relief arrived, and I wasted not a single moment making my way to the one female I could not stop thinking about.

We were not allowed to carry weapons off the grounds and locked mine away in the guard station, but my body was the only weapon I needed.

Even within the perimeter of allowed travel, I was an oddity. People stared. Cars slammed on their brakes. It had been obvious within a few minutes of my first exploration of the area there were no seven-foot-plus Earth people. If there were, I hadn't seen them. It was not easy for me to blend in, unlike the Everian who was also a guard in the evenings, or even the Viken who'd been transferred home last week. At least I spoke the language; fluency in English was a requirement to be stationed at this Earth center, since humans weren't given NPUs in infancy like newly born infants from other Coalition planets.

The first time I'd entered the ice cream store, I'd just stood there and breathed in the scent. Sugar and baked goods, vanilla and... fuck, her. Standing behind the counter, she'd looked at me, and I was done for.

Today, she smiled. "Hi, Jorik. What will it be this time? I have a new flavor that might interest you."

There was only one flavor that interested me, but I stepped forward, glad the shop was empty but for the two of us. "And what flavor is that?" Your wet pussy? Your soft skin? I'll take one of everything...

"Monster Mash." She laughed, teasing me. My beast growled *mine* and I agreed. Her dark eyes held warmth, no fear at me being almost twice her size. Since she walked by the Processing Center on her way to work, she'd seen various alien guards. Knew of them. Didn't cross the street in fear. But that was when we were safely at our posts. At work. Here, in her place of business, I was relieved I no longer frightened her.

I didn't. She smiled again. "It's Neapolitan with gummy bears for monsters. The kids love it."

When she turned, I nearly sighed in relief as the strange plastic rectangle affixed to her T-shirt came into view. One word was there, in bold black letters. Finally. A name. *Gabriela.*

"Thank you, Gabriela."

"How do you know my name?" Her grin was pure happiness, and my beast all but preened.

I pointed. "You wear it on the small white rectangle."

She looked down at her large breasts, a slight pink flush entering her cheeks as she looked back up at me—found me staring.

"Oh right, they're new. The owner just got them in."

I wanted to run my hand over her

sleek black hair, feel the strands between my fingers. I wanted to nuzzle my nose into her neck, breathe in her scent, lick the pulse point. Then lower... fuck, I wanted to lick my way down her body, drown in her softness, taste her very essence. No doubt she'd be slick and wet, all hot and sticky for me to lick right up. And as I ran my tongue along the top of the ice cream she'd handed me, I was not thinking about the food item. I'd put my tongue on her, swirl it around. Lick. Taste. Devour.

2

J orik

SHE TURNED bright red and her smile faded a bit as she turned away from me and found some busy work behind the counter.

I'd pushed her far enough for one day, I supposed. My beast growled in disagreement as I moved to sit down in a seat in the corner, far from both her and the door. I turned my chair so I could pretend not to notice as her glance wandered to me over and over. My beast fought me, hard, but I was not an animal. Not yet. I didn't want her afraid.

I wanted her hungry. Hot. Ready for my touch and my cock.

That first day, she'd offered me a hand-held food cone filled with vanilla ice cream. The next day, chocolate. Each day I visited, she gave me a new flavor. After weeks of visiting, I hadn't tried all the possibilities. I didn't give a shit about them. All I cared about was seeing her smile at my arrival, the brush of our fingers as she passed me the dessert which was meant to offer cooling relief from the hot Florida air.

I wouldn't cool. Not until she was mine. Until I sank into her, filled her with my seed. Claimed her.

I was content. For now. We talked; each day I learned more about her. An only child, she had lived in Florida her entire life. Her parents were dead, although she didn't share details of their demise. The ice cream store was not hers, she was the manager. Her dream was to own her own store, rather than work for another, although I learned she did not have the wealth to follow that passion.

This made her vulnerable. Working for another. Dependent on that human's attitude or whim. I did not like knowing my female was at the mercy of another for survival.

No. I would win her. Claim her. I would take care of her.

If she'd have me.

But not here. We could not mate and live on Earth. The human government would not allow such a union. She would need to be willing to leave Earth behind forever. Her life. Her neighbor's orange cat, whose photo was taped to the wall behind the register. I had discovered the creature was called Pumpkin—named after an Earth vegetable of the same color.

The fact that a scratching, hissing creature that killed small mammals and birds would be her favorite pet gave me hope that she could learn to love my beast as well.

If not for Gabriela—I loved knowing her name and rolled it around in my mind —I had no reason to return to Atlan. A few cousins were all the family I had. The promise of wealth and riches, estates awarded to a Warlord who had been lucky enough to survive both the Hive and his Mating Fever. I would be wealthy, if I returned home. I could care for her on Atlan, make her happy. Give her a palace and fine clothes, servants to clean the dishes, rather than see her hands rough and reddened from such hard work. I wanted to give her enough money to pursue her passion now. Here. But I had none. I was not paid in Earth funds and Atlan currency was meaningless here. We were given an odd, striped plastic card that the human retailers accepted for payments.

Money or not, her dreams became mine. I wanted to fulfill her desires. I knew. My beast knew.

She was mine and I would have her.

Nothing would stand in my way.

Content to simply be in the same space with her, I enjoyed the sensation of the cold little candy bears heating in my mouth and sticking to my teeth. We had nothing like this ice cream treat on Atlan, and I discovered a liking for the shocking combination of freeze and sweetness exploding on my tongue. I relaxed, exactly where I wanted to be.

The human criminal did not check the corner when he entered the store with the small weapon in his hand.

It would be his last mistake.

Humans called the primitive projectile firing weapon a gun. It was basic. Prone to misfiring. Loud and had limited range and shooting capabilities.

All in all, the small silver metal weapon was inferior in every way. But it could kill my female.

Gabriela saw him at once, and the look on my sweet female's face as she stood behind the machine that held

Earth money made my beast surge forward before I even thought to regain control. Her cheeks, usually flushed pink, went pale. Her eyes were wide and held fear. Her body shook and not with laughter.

I noticed this in the blink of an eye. The door was close to her position. Too close. In less than a second, the male gripped her shoulder with one hand. In the other, he held the gun to her forehead. They both stood behind the low counter where she normally accepted payment from customers.

Tall, for an Earth male, dark hair peeked out from his billed hat. An oversized T-shirt only accentuated how thin he was. I could snap him like a twig. Blue pants worn by most humans drooped about his waist. Markings covered both his arms. Tattoos, I'd learned, with odd pictures and images on them. He was much larger than Gabriela, his grip sure, his intent obvious.

"Jorik!" she cried, her eyes widening as

I approached. She was quaking, trying to tilt her head away from the gun. "Run."

Run? As in leave? Now? With her like this? Being threatened? My fists clenched at the thought of her trying to save me. Me! While I was dressed in my Coalition uniform, I wasn't armed. But I didn't need a weapon to help her.

His gun was nothing like an ion pistol, but I knew it could kill, especially pressed to her head. Earth was a primitive place. Without ReGen wands or pods, people died from bullet wounds all the time. My Gabriela could not survive such an injury.

My beast rose and I felt myself growing bigger, taller. Broader. This... this... asshole threatened what was mine?

When he saw me, his eyes widened.

I grinned. He might think to intimidate a small female, but he was no match for me. He could empty the entire contents of his primitive weapon into my body, and unless he blew a hole in my head, I'd still tear him in two.

"You dare threaten my woman?" I

asked, my voice half-growl because of my beast.

"This ain't about you." A sneer turned up the corner of his mouth. "I want money, and she's going to give it to me."

"You want nothing. You're already dead."

"No." He shook his head, as if any other outcome was an option. "I just want the money, man. No harm, no foul." As I neared, he shook even more violently than Gabriela. Still, he wasn't a complete fool. He kept the gun pressed to her skull, rather than pointed at me. The moment she was clear of that threat, he would die.

"You touched her, hold a gun to her head," I said, stating the obvious, and the reason he was going to die.

"You're one of those fucking aliens," he said, finally turning the gun to point at me. Not so smart after all.

My beast became more enraged, eager to end this. My skin stretched, my focus sharpened.

Kill. Maim. Destroy.

"I am." My voice was deeper, my beast taking over.

"Are you... are you growing?" His eyes raked over me, his hand shook.

I took a step toward him. "I am Atlan. Do you know what that means?"

He gave a jerky shake of his head, then pulled Gabriela in front of him. A human shield. She cried out at the action, her eyes closed tightly as a soft whimper of pain escaped. I knew he'd hurt her and I growled.

"It means I have an inner beast. One who doesn't like when my female is threatened."

"Beast?" he said. His brain processed my words, and he looked at Gabriela for a few seconds and then shoved her away. Hard.

She fell to the floor, landing with a loud thud behind the counter where I could no longer see her. She groaned, her breathing short and panicked.

Unacceptable.

"Beast," I repeated, all snarl. I was no

longer in control. My inner animal had taken over. I was fully transformed. One word was all I could manage.

The foolish human fired his weapon, the bullet moving through the air quickly, but not fast enough. My beast moved out of the way, and I reached out, ripped the gun from his hand, then ripped his screaming head from his body.

～

GABRIELA OLIVAS SILVA, *Miami, FL*

MY EARS RANG and I could hear Jorik's voice on the other side of the counter. Then the robber's.

The gun went off.

Then a scream—a terrible scream— cut short by the sound of... I didn't want to think about what that sound was. My head hurt too much where I'd whacked it on the counter on my way down. I was going to have a bump, but luckily, that seemed to be my only injury. I'd be fine if my heart wasn't beating so hard I feared it would explode right out of my chest.

A gun. That asshole had held a gun to my head. He could have... would have...

"Gabriela?"

Jorik's voice interrupted my panic attack, and I tried to sit up without looking like an idiot, which is what I felt like. That robber had been hanging around here, scoping out the joint, for the last two days. I'd known something was up yesterday when he came in early and asked to use the restroom. I should have said no. But he looked like he could use a break. Torn shirt. Ripped jeans. Shoes with a hole in the toe and mismatched laces. His hair had been dirty and unkempt. He looked homeless, which he probably was, and I'd always had a soft spot for broken things.

Animals, mainly. But I'd made an exception yesterday—and lived to regret it. Animals didn't lie, or cheat, or say mean things. They just did the best they could.

People, on the other hand? People were dangerous.

Apparently, so were aliens.

"Gabriela?" His hands were on me before I could get my bearings, lifting me off the dirty floor mats like I weighed no more than a feather.

Another laughable thought. I giggled, letting him pull me to my feet, then against his chest... which seemed... higher than it should be. I giggled again, knew my nearly hysterical outburst was due to some kind of shock, but I didn't care. Until I saw the blood. On Jorik. Not a lot, but that jerk had fired a gun at the big alien. Had Jorik been shot? For me?

"Jorik? Are you all right?" I shoved against him, but I might as well have been pushing at a two-ton brick wall. Sure, I was a big woman. I loved ice cream, and it showed... everywhere. But I couldn't budge him. "Let me go. You're hurt."

His laugh wasn't a laugh, really, but a rumble against my ear. "No. You hurt."

Blinking away my confusion, I won-

dered if I was hearing things, or if Jorik—
smiling, teasing, charming Jorik—had
suddenly lost the ability to speak in complete sentences. Maybe he was bleeding to
death. "Jorik, I'm serious. I need to make
sure you're all right."

"No. Where live? I take care you."

"Where do I live?" I repeated.

"Yes." I was cradled in his arms now,
his huge, huge hand coming up to press
my cheek to his chest when we walked by
what I assumed was the robber's dead
body. That was just fine with me. I didn't
want to see what that rending sound had
led to.

"My apartment is only a couple blocks
away. I'm fine. Put me down. I can walk."

"No."

Fine. The truth of the matter was I
didn't much feel like walking anyway. I
was still freaked out that I'd had a gun
pressed to my temple, an asshole had
been stalking me for the last two days,
and if Jorik hadn't come in when he did, I
could have been killed. That thought

made my heart race again, and I couldn't breathe, my chest too tight.

As if he could sense how I felt, Jorik's free hand stroked the side of my head and face, even as he walked. I felt like a pampered kitten and I didn't even want to fight. Jorik was big, strong, and sexy as hell. I knew he was a guard at the Bride Processing Center. I'd seen him stationed at the gates on most days when I walked to work. I had done enough research to know he was from a planet called Atlan. He was a beast —whatever that meant. But he didn't seem like a monster to me. He had black hair and dark skin, like a younger, bigger Dwayne Johnson. The Rock would be a good nickname for Jorik as well. And his eyes? Lord help me, his eyes were textbook bedroom eyes. All sex and teasing and secrets.

He'd been coming into the shop every day for the last few weeks, and I had begun to hope that it wasn't for the food.

But who was I to think such a thing? He was an alien warrior, trusted to guard one of the most important alien facilities on Earth. The processing center here in Miami was the hub for both Interstellar Brides and soldier recruitment for the Coalition Fleet. There were only seven sites in the world, and the aliens who ran them guarded them like they were made of pure gold.

I'd seen aliens from Prillon Prime, Atlan, and Everis—the ones who looked just like us. I knew there were more planets out there, but it seemed they liked to keep the freakishly huge or freakishly fast warriors on guard duty. I'd watched them, these warriors, Jorik most of all, as they wrestled or played their odd sport games within the walls of the compound. The Everians could move so fast I would lose track of them and reminded me of television vampires. The Prillon warriors were just... odd. Pointed features. Unusually colored skin. Copper. Bronze. Golden. Most of them had shades of gold or orange colored eyes as well. They were seven feet tall and could never pass for human.

But the Atlans? They looked like superstar football or basketball players. Seven feet or taller. Jorik was ridiculously tall, dark, and a walking temptation. They all looked like sex gods, all sculpted muscle and hungry stares. Jorik, especially, had the stare down. The stare that made me feel beautiful, instead of "plus-sized". The stare that made me want to strip naked and parade my body around in front of a male as if it were a feast for his senses rather than an embarrassment for me.

The. Stare.

He was giving it to me as he carried me to my apartment. He set me on my feet just long enough for me to pull the key from the front pocket of my shorts and unlock the door. The moment it swung open, he lifted me again. His shoulder was within reach this time, as if he'd gotten smaller on the walk, and I wondered what kind of crazy I was for thinking he'd been almost a foot taller in the store.

He kicked the door closed behind him, set me down on my feet, turned. "Lock it."

I raised a brow but did as he said. It made me feel safer, which was just dumb. Nothing would get through him. And anything that could would have no problem with the flimsy wooden door.

His grunt was accompanied by a hint of a grin, and I saw the charming man—alien—I'd grown comfortable talking to every day in the shop. The shop... "Shit. We have to call the police. The owner. Oh, my God. I shouldn't have left like that. She's going to be freaked. And what if customers come in?"

Want some pecan praline with that dead body?

I covered my face with my hands. "Oh, my God. What am I going to do?"

Jorik reached for me, to stop my pacing. I faced him and he lifted his hands, as if to touch my face. But his glance strayed from my eyes to his palms and he cursed in that strange language again. "I will not touch you again with blood on my hands."

Happy to focus on his problem instead of my own, I led him to the kitchen. The naughty part of me—the part full of ideas and wishful thinking—thought of taking him to the bathroom, stripping him naked, and squeezing together in my tiny shower. But that would involve a whole lot of skin and even more assumptions on my part.

Maybe the stare was just a normal, everyday look on an alien.

And maybe I was thinking this way because I'd almost died a few minutes ago. Maybe this was shock.

I watched as the most amazing, gorgeous hunk of male perfection I'd ever seen—in real life or digital—stripped out of his shirt in the middle of my tiny kitchen.

Definitely not shock. I wanted him. Had for a while. I thought about him all the time, wondered if he would appear in my shop every day, was ridiculously happy when he did.

He scrubbed his hands in my sink and he looked like what he was—foreign. I'd never had a man in this apartment, let alone one the size of Jorik. His head nearly reached the ceiling tiles and he had to duck under the one, ugly fluorescent light cover filled with half a dozen dead flies.

Embarrassing. But I hated flies, and I hated cleaning even more. By the time I left the ice cream shop spotless at the end of every shift, I just didn't have the energy to drag out a ladder and tackle that kind of thing.

Besides. Chest. There was chest. And shoulders. And oh, my god, his back. Muscles on muscles. An ass so tight it looked like two bowling balls were hiding under his pants. No one's ass could be that hard, could it? Every inch of me was soft, everything but my bones. The idea of anyone being that solid seemed surreal, and I reached out to touch...

I snatched my hand back. Nope.

"Jeez, what's wrong with me?" I whispered to myself as I swung away, tucked my hand safely against my side and made my way back to the door. Suddenly, double checking the deadbolt seemed like an excellent distraction from the temptation currently in my kitchen.

He washed up, the smell of dish soap and what I could only think of as him. Dark. Musky. Wild.

Fighting the urge to make a damn fool of myself, I pressed my forehead to the cool door panel and tried to think rationally. I should call my boss, the owner. She was a nice woman in her sixties who had given me a break when I needed one. She paid well and she was fair, so I'd stayed. For three years. I should call her. She would worry. She would call the police. No doubt they'd be pounding on my door soon enough. There was a security camera system at the store, so they would be able to rewind the video and find out exactly what happened. They'd want my statement. And Jorik's. We should take care of that. Like, now.

But I didn't want to. I didn't want to talk about it. I didn't want to even think about it. Like, ever. I wanted to press my naked breasts to Jorik's back, bury my nose in his skin and breathe him in. I wanted to lick him up one side and down the other, kiss him, taste him, and ride his cock until I couldn't think straight. I wanted to have mind-blowing, amazing sex with someone I was actually attracted to for the first time in my life. No fumbling hands. No lies. No manipulation. No games. Just raw animal lust.

And that was insane because all we'd done was talk. I'd hand him a new flavor of ice cream, we'd chat as he ate the cone, then he would leave. I knew little about him and it wasn't like he was from Kansas or California. He was from another planet. What could we have in common? What made me interested in him? Oh yeah, he was hot and it seemed I had an inner sex fiend wanting to come out.

I wanted to be an animal, at least once in my life. I wanted to have the kind of kinky, hot sex I read about in my favorite books.

I wanted Jorik. Over me. Inside me. Touching me. Making me come until I couldn't think at all.

3

*G*abriela

"ARE YOU ALL RIGHT?"

Jorik was right behind me. He didn't touch me, but he was so close I could feel the heat radiating off him.

I nodded but continued to stare at the door. Afraid to move. Afraid if I turned around, I'd jump him. Or worse... he'd leave. They always left, in the end.

"Gabriela," he said. "I must touch you."

Oh god, that voice. Those words. Was I hearing things? He'd called me his female in the store. I'd heard that. Not my imagination. Right?

I closed my eyes and gently banged my forehead against the cool surface of the door. It had to be the stress. I was nowhere near hot enough for this gorgeous man—alien—to want me like that. I had long black hair. Straight. No curl. Boring. My skin was good, the Latino heritage from my parents making my clear brown skin my best feature. But after that? No. I was a solid ten sizes above fashionable and hadn't been touched by a boy since high school.

Not that I didn't have needs. My inner kink was alive and well—just lonely. It's just that taking a spin with B-O-B—my *battery activated boyfriend*—a couple times a week was a lot easier than having my heart broken over and over... and over.

"Maybe you should go, Jorik. I don't think—I..."

"Please, Gabriela. I need to touch you."

"What do you mean?" Not hallucinating. He'd actually...

He leaned down, the fan of his breath a warm caress on my neck. "You are so beautiful, Gabriela. So soft. I can't hold back any longer. I must feel you beneath my fingers. My lips. Learn every inch of you. What pleases you, what makes you whimper."

He kissed my cheek, bending way, way down to do it. Holy shit, he was huge. I wondered if his cock was as big as the rest of him.

"Writhe."

Goose bumps broke out on my skin. His voice. God. It was so deep, it rumbled through my chest. My nipples were hard as rocks, pressing against my bra.

"Beg."

"Jorik," I said.

"My beast can't hold back any longer. We must have you."

My panties were ruined, just because of his words. His inner beast was about to be introduced to mine—except she was half-starved and very fucking naughty.

"Yes," I whispered, still afraid to turn around.

That didn't deter him, for his hands went to my waist as his mouth settled on my neck, kissing, licking, sucking at that tender flesh.

I gasped at the contact, at his... voraciousness. His hands moved, roved over me. Hips to belly, waist to breasts, back to my hips and down my thighs, up and over my pussy. They didn't stop moving, just learned me.

I heated at the contact, going molten. Soft. My palms pressed into the door, my forehead pressing into the cool surface.

"Jorik," I said again, this time all breathy.

He was turning me on unlike anyone

before him, and I was still fully clothed. God, could I come from just this?

I heard a rumble, almost a growl. With my head tipped down, I watched as he dropped to his knees behind me. His hands dropped to my ankles then slid up the outside of my legs, over my shorts, to my stomach. From there, he moved up, cupping my large breasts through my bra and T-shirt. "I want you naked, Gabriela. I want to touch you everywhere. Taste you. Fill you with my cock. Make you come over and over again."

He rolled my hard nipples in both of his hands and I moaned, pressing into the touch. No one should be able to do this to me with my clothes on. I couldn't even think. All I could do was want. "Yes. Yes. Everything."

I felt a shudder pass through him where he'd pressed his head to my back, his chest to my ass, his hands—were shaking.

Had I done that to him? Was he as

mindless and desperate as I? Did he need me to touch him? Kiss him? Taste him?

I turned in his arms so my back was to the door. Even on his knees, his face was nearly even with mine. God, he was huge. His dark eyes were glazed with lust and something else, something I'd never seen on a man's face before and couldn't hope to name. Didn't dare, not when it looked so much like—reverence. Like worship.

Like love.

But that was impossible. Wasn't it? I barely knew him.

He froze as I lifted my hands to his face, cupped his cheek, traced his lower lip with my thumb. He was beautiful. Truly beautiful. "I'm going to kiss you now." Why I made the announcement, I had no idea, but I felt like I needed to give him fair warning, as if he needed to brace himself. Maintain control. Mentally prepare for an onslaught to the senses that would put him over the edge.

I shuddered. Or maybe the warning was for me. I didn't do this. I didn't have sex with strangers. I didn't have sex with aliens. Hell, I didn't have sex. I never felt comfortable with my body, hated looking in the mirror. That I wanted to strip naked and give anyone all of me was so foreign to my being I was having trouble making sense of the moment.

But I wasn't going to waste this opportunity either. Jorik was gorgeous. Rockstar, movie star, sex god beautiful. And for whatever reason, he seemed to want this just as much as I did.

Lowering my head, slowly, so slowly, I stared into his eyes as I got closer. Closer. Closing them the briefest moment before my lips touched his.

He let me have my way, his huge hands resting on my hips, unmoving, as I explored and tasted. God, he tasted good. Indescribable. Perfect.

When I slipped my tongue into his mouth, he moved, tugging at my shorts until I wiggled out of them. Eager for some skin on skin action, I pulled my T-shirt off over my head until I stood before him in my panties and bra.

He looked his fill, taking in every inch of me. I waited for some sign of disappointment, but there was none. If anything, his gaze grew darker, more heated.

Was he real?

I reached for him.

"No. Don't move." He pressed a flat palm to the center of my chest and held me pressed to the door. So dominant. So fucking hot. I whimpered.

Move? I could barely breathe.

His free hand slid up my bare thigh. Thank god I put on cute silk panties this morning and not the *it's-laundry-day-granny-panties.*

But my hips. My stomach. My huge breasts. Everything was sticking out, was right there in front of his face. He was still. Unmoving. Did he dislike what he saw? I had cellulite, a little jiggle. Did he—

"Look at you. Gorgeous." He leaned forward and pressed a kiss to the center of my stomach, held himself there as if he were trying to breathe me in.

I exhaled, not realizing I'd held my breath. My panties were tugged down over my hips and around my ankles in less than a second. I gasped when he tilted me to the side just enough to sink his teeth into one cheek of my bottom.

"Jorik!" I cried. It wasn't a hard bite, more like a nibble. A big nibble.

I wiggled my hips, turned on beyond belief. He groaned.

"This." I felt the brush of a finger along my slit and still couldn't move, pinned to the door as I was. "You are wet. Ready."

He used his fingers to part the lips of my pussy and I felt cool air. There. I licked my lips, tried to breathe, but I was so turned on. What was he doing? I'd expected to be tossed on the floor, fucked hard and thoroughly. A quickie. But this?

I wasn't going to survive this.

I heard his deep breath. "Your scent. My beast likes your scent. Will he like your taste? I've wondered if you are sweet everywhere, what your pussy tastes like."

I had no idea aliens were dirty talkers. And I didn't know I got off on word porn. He'd only nuzzled me with his nose and had roaming hands. Bit my ass. That was all and I was close to coming.

A hand hooked about my hip and pulled my hips forward as his mouth found my center.

I cried out at the feel of him licking me from front to back. Then again. Like an ice cream cone.

"Oh my god," I groaned when he did something magical with his tongue on my clit.

A finger slid into my pussy, curled. Fucked me slowly. He was in no rush, his pace methodical as if he had all the time in the world. "Quickie" didn't seem to be in the Atlan language.

"Jorik, please," I begged. Oh yes, I begged. It was too much, too good, and I couldn't even see him.

Jorik moved the hand from my chest

to roll a nipple between his fingers, then squeeze my breast, tugging on the entire thing until my knees shook, ready to collapse. "My beast is busy, Gabriela. Your begging is not necessary. We will see to you."

Now two fingers were inside me as he worked my clit.

He was good. So, so good. I'd had a guy go down on me before, but it hadn't done much for me. Now I knew why. He'd had no idea what he'd been doing. I wasn't even sure now if he'd actually found my clit.

But Jorik? God, Jorik was an oral god.

I cried out his name again, wiggled my hips so I was probably smothering him with my pussy, but I didn't care. He made me this way. If he wanted to breathe, he could make me come.

He didn't just find my clit, he claimed it. Owned it. Sucked the small, sensitive bit of flesh into his mouth and worked me with his tongue as he fucked me with his fingers. The suction motion, so fast, so hard, made me writhe, my hands on his shoulders. I pressed forward, needed more. And he gave me what I wanted. One motion of his tongue and curl of his fingers. Some magical combination of press and flick and I went off like the fireworks at Fourth of July.

My fingernails dug into his shoulders, my knees buckled, but he didn't relent, working me. Fucking me with his fingers. His fingers were replaced with his tongue and he slipped one wiggling digit just inside my ass, the foreign feeling adding to the overwhelming flood of sensation roaring through my body like a hurricane. He pushed me, filled me, licked me and touched me until I came a second time, unable to stand. Unable to speak. I could barely breathe. For the first time in my life, I was a hot mess.

"More," I said, just before I leaned in and kissed him. My arms went about his neck as our tongues tangled. I tasted him, and me.

He pushed me back and stared where

my breasts hung heavy. He actually growled, the sound making me laugh. Actually laugh.

I took the opportunity to look him over since he wasn't wearing a shirt, all dark skin, hard muscles. He had a bit of hair on his chest, and I wanted to touch every inch of him, run my hands though all of it. Pet him. Make him purr. He was big. God, I could take hours going over every inch of him. Then I saw the bulge in his pants and realized his cock had a lot of inches. It was like there was a pipe in his pants. It angled up and to the side as if trying to work its way out of his prison.

My inner walls clenched wondering how he was going to fit.

His gaze tipped down to see what I was looking at. His hands opened his pants and his cock fell into his waiting palm.

"Oh my god. You are a beast."

He laughed then as he stroked himself. Thick and long, it was darker than the skin on his chest, the head flared wide.

I wanted it. I ached to get on that thing. Ride it.

I licked my lips, wanting to do too many things at once.

When I glanced back up, I found him watching me. Waiting. This was my call. He was huge, but I was in control.

And that knowledge made me feel safe, set me off like a rocket.

Fuck. I was going to come again.

I pushed gently on his chest, confident he would go where I directed, and he did. Settling into a seated position on the soft rug I had in the living room, his legs straight out in front of him so I could straddle his thighs. So I did, settling into his lap so we were chest to chest, my thighs atop his. He still had his pants on, but I wasn't as patient as he seemed to be. His cock was out and that was what I wanted.

"I need you," I admitted, lifting up so I hovered over his hard length.

His eyes met mine, held. I wiggled my

hips until I had the tip of his cock pressed to my entrance.

"Jorik," I breathed. "Please. I want you inside me."

"Mine," he replied, settling his hands on my hips and pushing me down onto him.

"Oh!"

He was big. Like huge. I was stretched wide, opened up. Filled. Crammed. My pussy was still swollen from his attention, and the sensitive flesh wrapped around him like a fist, squeezing him as we both groaned. My inner muscles rippled and quivered around him like aftershocks from an orgasm, pushing toward another release.

Jorik groaned, pulled my body forward until my clit rested against his abdomen, my pussy open wide, my body spread open and totally his. He bottomed out inside me and I felt the rumble from his chest and into mine.

My feet were on the floor as I straddled him, and I began to lift and lower.

Deeper, harder, faster. All the while, he helped, lifting and lowering, thrusting his hips up so we slapped together.

I fucked myself on him, all but using him for my pleasure. But I wasn't alone in this. Sweat dotted his forehead, his mouth turned into a snarl. His hands began to move over me, cupping my breasts, playing with my nipples, pinching and squeezing my ass, pulling me open from behind so he could slide a bit deeper as I rode him.

His finger found my ass and he stroked over the outside, teasing me with his touch. Making my pussy clench and spasm in reaction. Everything went tight.

"Jorik, I'm... oh god, I'm coming!"

I couldn't hold back if I tried, the orgasm so different than the ones he'd given me with his mouth. Places inside me, the ones I was rubbing and nudging with a huge cock, filled me with a pleasure I didn't know existed.

As I came, all I could hear from him was *mine, mine, mine*. His hands tightened, his cock thickened and he shouted, some foreign word, as I felt his seed fill me. So deep.

I could barely catch my breath as he held me secure. I'd come, fallen hard, but he'd held me through it. Kept me safe.

I opened my eyes, looked up at him once the clinging desperation of my orgasm faded. I shifted, but he was still thick and hard within me, even as I felt his seed slip out, slide down our joined thighs.

"You're... you're still hard."

He grinned, quick and lethal, then flipped us so I was on my back and he loomed over me. Our connection wasn't broken with the motion, his cock still embedded deep.

"I'm not done," he replied, then began to move.

"Oh!"

Yes, the Atlan beast was a patient lover. I'd been the needy, frantic one. He'd let me set the pace the first time, but now, with him holding his weight off me with his forearms, with him watching me as he fucked me with his beast-sized cock, I was at his mercy.

"You're coated in my seed. My beast is happy knowing you are marked."

Marked? So primitive. God, I was being fucked by a caveman.

"We have only begun, Gabriela."

That was the last thing he said before he set to his task. Fucking me. *Marking* me.

We barely knew each other and yet the connection was incredible. I didn't just feel fucked, I felt... possessed. Claimed.

And when I came another time, he was right there with me, burying himself so deep I didn't know where he stopped and I began.

He was still hard after he came again. We were sweaty and messy, cum everywhere, but I didn't care. He was ready for more and my pussy... it ached, not from discomfort, but from want.

The only thing that kept us from continuing was a funny beeping. He pulled out of me after it didn't stop after a minute. I whimpered at the emptiness I felt as he reached for his pants, grabbed a device that looked like a strange cell phone.

"Jorik," he said, speaking into it.

The response came through loud and clear, on some kind of speaker. "Warlord Jorik, report to Center Commander Captain Gades immediately. The human police have issued a warrant for your arrest. Do not surrender to them. Make your way here without incident. That's an order."

"I need more time, Sir." He looked to me, probably seeing a woman well-fucked, naked and with little love bites, red marks from whiskers, a very well-used pussy. Seed coating my thighs. I looked to his cock. Still hard, glistening with our joined fluids.

"You will return now, Warlord. You ripped the head off a human and they caught it on their primitive vid feeds. This is one hell of a diplomatic mess. Get your ass back here now or a team of guards will be sent to your location for extraction."

"Yes, Sir." Jorik tossed the communication device onto the carpet and I watched him dress. He said nothing. What was there to say? Thanks for the fuck?

But the conversation confirmed what I'd already known. Jorik had killed that man to protect me. And as much as I'd been taught my entire life that killing was wrong, I was still grateful he'd done it. "Jorik?"

He turned to me, fully clothed, the alien warrior once more. "You are mine, Gabriela. Remain here. I will handle the authorities."

He leaned down and kissed me, just once, but his touch was gentle, his soft lips lingered. He placed a warm palm on my abdomen as he kissed me, as if he couldn't get enough.

"Gods be damned, you are pure temptation, female. So soft." He ran his hand over my body, hip to neck, and I lay there like a pet kitten and reveled in his touch.

"Are you coming back?" It was weak to ask. Stupid. I regretted the words the moment they came flying out of my mouth. But Jorik kissed me again, then stood.

"This is not finished between us, Gabriela. You are mine, now."

Mine. He'd said it multiple times while we were fucking, but hearing it from a fully dressed, logical male was different.

It felt right. I could be his if it meant more loving like this. My swollen, sated pussy and tender breasts agreed. More would be good. A lot more.

I smiled as he walked out the door. I believed he'd come back to me. I was the flavor he wanted to taste again. And again.

The latch clicked, and I rolled onto my side, a silly, stupid grin on my face. I was falling in love—no—scratch that—I was already in love with an alien. A freaking alien.

And I had no trouble using his limited vocabulary to stake a claim of my own.

"Mine."

4

J orik, Coalition Fleet Processing Center, One Hour Later

"IT'S UNACCEPTABLE, WARLORD," the center commander said, slapping her hand on the table. A Prillon and close to my height, she had to lean forward to do so. "What were you thinking?"

I sat, arms folded over my chest, stared. I didn't care. My beast prowled within but wasn't fazed. "My mate was in danger," I said, for the third time.

Her golden stare met mine. Held. I

might be bigger, but she was not intimidated. I wasn't the first Atlan she'd dealt with and wouldn't be the last. And I had a feeling Atlans were easier for her to comprehend than the humans she had to work with on a daily basis. "Your mate? I don't see mating cuffs on those wrists. And there's no record of you receiving a match, or even being processed in the Interstellar Brides Program. What the fuck were you thinking, grabbing some random Earth female off the street? Are you suffering from Mating Fever?"

Her gaze raked over me.

"No."

"And yet you wish to claim an unauthorized match with a female? Do you even know how much trouble you've caused me? You pulled a man's head from his body and the humans caught it all on vid feed."

I shrugged. "I would do it again. He deserved to die. He was threatening my mate." My mate. Gabriela. I thought of our time together... every moment. The sight of her body, the feel of her skin, the taste of it. Her scent. It was all burned into my memory. My beast, thankfully, was soothed by the knowledge she'd been pleasured, that my seed marked her. Filled her, even now.

She shook her head, sighed. "No, Warlord. You were dispensing justice for a human crime. You have not only disregarded the laws which govern this planet, you committed what is, in their eyes, a crime punishable by life in prison."

I sat up straight. "What?" That got my attention. What the fuck was she talking about? "I protected my mate. That is all."

"No, you took a human who wanted to take some money—not even this female's personal wealth, but her employer's—he wished to remove money from the store and leave. And you killed him." She leaned against the edge of her desk now, her second resigned sigh scaring me more than a reprimand ever could. "You are being charged with one of their worst crimes, murder in the second degree, Jorik."

"I don't know what that means."

"You know the word *murder*?" she countered, the tone laced with sarcasm.

I pressed my lips together as I knew she wasn't seeking an answer.

"As this center is considered an international embassy, you are safe here. They can't come and drag you out of here to their prison, their court system. Their... primitive form of justice. You are safe, for the moment. But I have extradition papers waiting for me in the front office. Once I see them, I can't protect you without causing an Interplanetary Incident. Prime Nial would need to get involved, as would the Atlans."

Fuck. "The law clearly states that any male may kill in defense of his mate."

"That's Coalition law, Jorik," she countered. "Not human."

"They are part of the Coalition now, are they not?" I waved my hand in the air indicating this entire, backwards planet.

"Yes, but you were not on Coalition property when you protected your mate. And by human law, she isn't your mate. You aren't legally married. You committed a human crime on a human. You were in the human city. Their territory. Their laws." Her frown was full of pity and her voice had lost that snappy edge. Now she was just prompting me to what I'd done wrong. She sympathized, I could tell, but she had a shitty job and again, had to play by the humans' rules.

I'd barely said goodbye to Gabriela before I left her small quarters at the center commander's request. I'd come peacefully, although not happily, for I was not eager to leave my mate. I was not ashamed of what we'd done. The opposite, in fact. I was proud. Honored she would be mine. That what we'd shared had been so... perfect. She now knew I'd do anything for her, to protect her from danger, and to cherish every inch of her body with my own. I would return to her. Or she would come to me. The human laws would not be allowed to separate us.

"I will not leave my mate."

"You do not wear mating cuffs." The commander spoke quietly. I'd heard the steel in her tone before. I was fucked. "You are not afflicted with Mating Fever. Have you even asked this female to be your mate?"

Fuck. "No, but I—we—" What could I say without dishonoring my female? "She has given me her body. We have been together."

She didn't even blink. "Yet, you have not officially claimed her."

"I have not claimed her, but she is mine," I said through gritted teeth.

She laughed, although without any humor. "Welcome to Earth, Warlord. You've assimilated well, but humans do not place the same reverence on intimate acts that we do. She is not yours. What you did was commonly referred to as a one-night-stand, in human slang."

"It was not one night," I countered,

settling back and crossing my arms once again. I felt like brooding, for no matter what I seemed to say, she didn't understand. "It was this morning... and we did not stand." Not while I was fucking her, at least. She stood, as I held her in place and worked her with my tongue. I smelled of Gabriela, of fucking. Her scent clung to me even now. Perhaps that was why my beast wasn't jumping over the table to throttle the female in charge so I could be done with this scolding and return to my mate.

The center commander's demeanor was as crisp as her dark Coalition uniform. Her arms went over her chest to mimic mine. "There are no rules against fraternizing with humans, so you have not broken Coalition laws. There is the problem of the *human* laws. They have very distinct rules about ripping a human's head off."

I thought of the male who threatened Gabriela. I would see the crazed look on his face for the rest of my life. I, too, would see my mate's fear. The look in her eyes had made my blood boil then, my beast awakened, and it did now, remembering. "He deserved it," I growled. "He had a primitive Earth weapon pointed at my mate."

This time, the center commander didn't correct my usage of mate. "I don't disagree, but you've placed the entire Coalition in a very delicate position. The human governments do not fully trust us. Not yet. We have irrational humans walking up and down the sidewalks out front with their ridiculous signs about us being the aliens. They are scared, Warlord. Terrified. They are small. Fragile."

Her words had me relaxing, until she continued.

"The comms footage provided by the business owner shows what happened, how you defended the Earth female."

I sat up, nodded. Even smiled. "Good, then they will know I committed no crime. I will return to my mate." And sink into her body once again. Pleasure her until she was too sated, too satisfied to do more than sleep in my arms.

She held up her hand to stop me. "No. The human news media is not playing that portion of the video to the public. They are only showing an Atlan in beast mode tearing the head off a man's body with his bare hands. The number of humans outside, protesting our presence, has tripled in the last hour."

"I protected my female, Commander," I repeated. Again.

"I understand. That is why you are being reassigned to Sector 437 effective immediately. You will proceed directly to transport as soon as this meeting is complete."

I stood so quickly my chair skidded backward, then tipped over. "What? Reassigned?"

"Miami police have a human with his head missing. To them, it was not self-defense since you, at the time, were an eight-foot alien beast. If they have their way, you will be locked up in one of their prisons for the rest of your life. The comms replay is evidence enough to prove your guilt, but the political firestorm you have created will make it impossible for you to receive a fair trial."

"Summon my female. I will take her to Atlan." My fists were clenched and my beast snarled.

She pursed her lips. "I'm afraid that's not possible. Per Coalition law, you have service time remaining on your military contract. Unless you are suffering from Mating Fever, you must serve the remainder of it before you earn the privilege of claiming a mate."

I looked to her neck, which held no collar. "You are not mated."

"No."

"When you are, you will understand," I explained. "I will not leave her."

"You will," her voice was cold. An order, not a request. "The people of this city will panic if they think a wild beast is going to rip their heads off, especially in a place like an ice cream store. *Children* go there."

"As if I were a threat to children," I told her. I ran my hand over the back of my neck. "The idea is ridiculous, but clearly humans don't see it that way. I'm their best ally. I would see anyone harming a child minus a head."

"Exactly." She sighed. "There is delicate political balance with having us here, Warlord, and you tipped it."

I shrugged. Again, I didn't care. From the look of her, she didn't either, but was frustrated more by the politics of dealing with humans and their archaic rules than with what I'd done. And now I was a political pawn.

"I am on your side, Warlord. I am trying to help you. If you remain, you will be arrested and put on trial for murder in the human courts. The Coalition will have to deal with months, if not years, of media frenzy and fear. If you are gone, this human circus ends today. The human Senator used his primitive telephone to call me himself. He needs the humans to know you are gone so they can sleep soundly."

I harrumphed. "I would think they would be comforted to know the bastard I killed is no longer a threat."

She didn't answer. Instead, she said, "This is Earth, Warlord. The rules are theirs."

"Then I will take my mate with me," I repeated.

"She is not your mate."

"She is my bride," I countered.

She shook her head. "She is not. You have not earned the honor of claiming one."

The rules stated a soldier in the Coalition fleet could be tested for a bride only after they'd completed their military service. My eyes widened as what she was telling me was finally becoming crystal clear, even though she'd said it aloud a little while ago. She intended for me to transport from Earth immediately without Gabriela, without even saying goodbye.

"I must go to space and serve the remainder of my time in the Coalition, then I can return for her?"

She sighed. "You are going to space. Permanently. You have been banned from this planet."

Banned—

"But my mate!" I said, my beast beginning to prowl.

"It would serve you best if you forgot about Gabriela Olivas Silva."

Forget about Gabriela?

"No." Rage took over, the beast grew. I saw red, felt my skin prickle, felt myself grow taller. "Mine."

I heard the center commander shout into the comms, saw two guards enter the room, ion blasters raised. I felt the chairs beneath my hands as I tossed them about the room. Gabriela was mine. I would not leave her behind. I could not be separated. I would not *forget.* One taste, one touch, one breathy scream as she found her pleasure on my cock and I knew.

"I. Will. Have. Her," I growled, tipping the table on its side.

My thoughts were of Gabriela. Her sleek hair, her lush curves. Then I felt the sizzle of a stun shot from an ion pistol. I was frozen in place, but the beast within continued to prowl.

"Get a transport beacon immediately, coordinates loaded for Sector 437. Warlord Wulf can handle him." The center commander came over to me, stood directly before me. We were no longer the same height since I was now taller with my beast in control. "I'm sorry it has to be this way, but once you are charging the Hive on an Atlan battlefield, you will forget about this woman, about Earth. Trust me. Wulf has suffered, as you now do. He will help you cope with your beast."

I watched as a guard ran back into the room, handed the small mobile transport device to his commanding officer.

No! That small dot would take me from Gabriela. I couldn't move. I couldn't resist.

Fuck!

The beacon was slapped to my chest and it beeped, signaling a countdown. Clearly, the center commander didn't want to be transported with me. She and the others stepped back, and I felt the sizzle of transport.

No. *No!*

I blinked, then again. I was standing on a transport pad on one of the battleships. I knew not which one. I didn't care. I wasn't on Earth.

Literally, in the blink of an eye, Gabriela was light years away.

I wasn't stunned anymore, but there was nowhere to go. No way to get back to Earth.

"Warlord Jorik."

I turned and saw a giant of an Atlan. I knew who I faced, even before he told me his name. And I knew where I was.

"Welcome to Battleship Karter, Jorik. I am Commander Wulf."

I circled the transport pad, as if there were some way I could find to return. "I need to go back. My mate is on Earth."

The giant warrior frowned and checked a data pad on his forearm. I was normal sized, for an Atlan. But Wulf? He made me feel small. No wonder he was feared in nearly every sector of space and infamous on the home planet. If he ever retired, he'd go home a god.

"She's my mate, Wulf." I pleaded with this Atlan male to understand, to help me. "I have to get back to her. I need her."

Wulf looked from the data to me. "Nothing here about a mate."

I felt the beast move through me, my bones crack, my face grow once again. The growl that came from my throat was more howl than words. "She's mine."

Unfazed, the commander stared at me, assessing. I should have been surprised when he showed no fear in reaction to my beast, but I had heard enough about Wulf to suspect he could put me down, even without using his beast. The bastard was fucking big enough.

My beast grew frantic at his lack of response. Someone was going to listen to me and send me back, if I had to tear this ship into a thousand pieces with my bare hands.

"I. Must. Go. Back."

Wulf couldn't miss my mood, my desperation. "All right. Calm down." That fast my beast settled.

"Mine. Gabriela. Mine."

Wulf nodded. "Fine. I'll take it up with Commander Karter when we return from our mission. He can contact Warden Egara on Earth. If your female agrees, he'll figure something out."

I could speak again. I could think again. Finally, someone was listening to me. And I had no doubt that Gabriela would agree to come to me. I'd left her sated and well taken care of. Protected. She'd screamed my name, come on my cock. She was mine. "She is mine," I said aloud so Wulf knew.

"Enough. Come on. You need to gear up. We're hitting Latiri 4 in two hours, and clearly, you need to work off some aggression."

Killing Hive for a few hours did sound appealing. Perhaps, next time I spoke to the commander on Earth, I wouldn't lose my temper. And I could think of nothing better than ripping my way through a few dozen Hive Soldiers, coming back tired and having Gabriela transport here so I could sink into the soft, hot welcome of her, my chosen female. "Let's go."

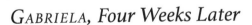

GABRIELA, *Four Weeks Later*

"I'M SORRY, ma'am, but I can't allow you to enter the premises." The stern guard stood blocking the entrance to the Processing Center. He wasn't nearly as big as

Jorik, and definitely human, but he was still intense.

I walked by every day I went to work... twice, and I'd never stopped before. I'd never needed to. But I was getting desperate.

It had been four weeks and three days since Jorik and I were together in my apartment. Four weeks and three days since he received his summons back to the center and then disappeared. I'd walked by the next day hoping to see him, talk to him, make plans to be together again, but he wasn't on duty. I walked by the day after that and he still wasn't on duty. I hadn't seen him since.

I had to wonder if I'd been a quick tumble, a human conquest tale for an alien to share with his buddies. But Jorik wasn't like that. He'd come into the store often, and I knew it wasn't for the ice cream. He'd been there for me. And then he'd saved me from that robber. I shivered, even now, at the thought of what could have happened.

"I need to speak to someone who works here," I told him.

"You want to volunteer as a bride?" he asked, looking me over.

The sun was hot today and sweat made my Sweet Treats T-shirt cling to my back. My hair was damp at my temples and I felt queasy. I needed to get out of the heat, but I had to find out about Jorik first.

Fortunately, after the robbery, I hadn't been fired. The incident had been on the news, but the alien head ripping had been the main theme. I'd tried to avoid it, but the internet was a cruel place, and my own curiosity crueler. The new stations had blurred the gory bits, but the true footage leaked. I saw it. Hell, by now I figured everyone on the planet had seen the terrifying look on Jorik's face when he'd killed the robber.

But I knew the truth. He'd done it for me. To protect me.

I wasn't afraid of what he'd done. I still wasn't afraid when I'd seen it replayed in that video. It made me feel... safe. Which was weird and made me miss Jorik. Without him, I felt so alone. Between that and the heat, my nausea rose, and I couldn't stop the waterworks. "Please, you have to let me in."

I had to see Jorik. I had to know what had happened to him. And even if he didn't want me anymore—the thought made me sob harder—he deserved the truth. He had said *mine* over and over again when we'd been together. He was very possessive. Ridiculously protective. He'd taken a man's head off with the same hands that had caressed my breasts, that had brought me to climax more than once.

He was ruthless, but also gentle. And he was mine.

God, I wanted him. Missed him. And now, after what I'd discovered a few weeks ago, I needed him.

It couldn't just be a quick fuck for me, for in our passion-hazed minds, we hadn't used protection—not that there were any condoms on Earth that would have fit

Jorik's huge cock. The deed was done. I was pregnant. Four tests had proven it.

"Brides have to be registered on the opposite side of the building, miss. You'll need to go to the main entrance. This entrance is for staff only."

I shook my head. "No, I'm not volunteering," I told the man who was patiently waiting for my answer. I didn't need to become a bride. I had the alien I wanted. Or, I wanted the alien I had.

"Then, ma'am, like I said, you can't enter." He held up his hand as if I were going to run past him.

I closed my eyes, took a deep breath.

"I'm... friends with Warlord Jorik," I said, trying a different strategy. "He was a guard here, like you."

The man relaxed his bearing, the corner of his mouth turning up into the semblance of a smile. "I'm new here, only two weeks. I don't know any Warlord Jorik."

"He's Atlan, at least seven feet tall." I raised my hand up in the air as if to show his height, which only made me look like I was measuring a giraffe. "Dark hair, dark complexion."

He shook his head. "Sorry."

"Can you ask someone then? I don't have to come in. I just need some questions answered."

A woman walked up, ready for work, held out her badge for the guard to inspect. She had dark hair pulled back in a sleek bun at the nape of her neck. Her Interstellar Brides uniform, a skirt, white blouse and jacket, were crisp and unwilted in the South Florida humidity.

"Perhaps I can help," she said, turning to me with a smile. "I'm Warden Egara."

I smiled back, wrung my hands. "Gabriela Silva."

"You have questions about being a bride?" she asked, a dark brow arching.

I shook my head. "No, about an Atlan who works here."

She looked me over in an efficient manner. "Why don't you come in with me where it's cool. I'll see if I can help." She flicked a glance at the guard, who nodded.

We entered the cool building and she led me into a small office. "Have a seat."

The air conditioning felt good, and I was glad to sit down. Pregnancy was weird. All my life I'd been used to the wet blanket of humidity that settled over Florida, but now, I could barely tolerate it. If it weren't for the tests I'd taken, I'd wonder if I were going through menopause with the hot flashes. The sweating. The lightheadedness.

She sat across from me at her desk. There were no papers upon it, only a tablet, nothing out of place. The room was sparse, the walls white. The only adornment was a huge IBP logo on the wall behind her. "Are you feeling all right?" she asked.

I nodded, no intention of telling her about the baby. If she knew, would they try to take the baby? Force me to undergo some weird alien testing? Without Jorik, I didn't want to take the chance that something would go wrong. I was still sweating and my skin was probably changing from flushed to green and back again as I went from overheated to nauseated and back again. "Yes, I should have worn a skirt today instead of jeans."

A thin excuse, but she bought it.

"So, how can I help?" she asked. "You have questions about an Atlan?"

God, was she really going to help me? "Yes, I've been trying to track down Warlord Jorik. He is a guard here."

"The guards are not mine. They serve under the CFPC Commander, the Coalition Fleet side." She lifted her hand. "This wing is reserved for the Brides Program."

"Oh," I murmured, looking down at my lap. Another dead end.

"But I can look into this for you."

My head whipped up to look her in the eye. "Thank you. I've been trying to find out about him for a month now. He and I have become... friends and he was called back here to the center after he saved my life. I never saw him again. I've come by the gate on my way to work, but the guards don't share information."

She gave a slight nod. "They aren't supposed to."

"Yes, I've learned that. I've also called several times. Been transferred, but no one is giving me any information."

She frowned. "Why do you want to know about him?"

"I..." I wasn't going to tell her we had sex, that we had a connection, a thing. I didn't think she'd understand. She was human, but still. I probably wasn't the first love-struck woman to stalk an alien. "I was the woman from the ice cream store. He was there and saved me from the robber."

She glanced at my T-shirt and got the confirmation she needed. "Ah, yes. I heard about that. I'm glad you're all right."

I pasted on a smile. "Yes, well, it's all because of Jorik and... and I wanted to thank him."

I also wanted to crawl into his arms and have him tell me that having an alien baby was no big deal, that I'd be fine. That he'd be with me every step of the way and I wouldn't be raising this baby alone. And when he'd held me, made me feel safe again, like everything was right in the world, I'd jump him and take his cock for a ride, but I kept that to myself.

She moved her tablet in front of her, swiped the screen. I waited quietly as she did...

"Warlord Jorik." She spelled his name aloud as she kept working her tablet. "Guard duty." Her hand stilled, but she continued to look at the screen.

Finally, she lifted her head. "Gabriela, Warlord Jorik was charged with second degree murder by the District Attorney here in Miami."

I gasped.

"To avoid criminal proceedings and an interplanetary media circus, he was reassigned. He's no longer on Earth."

"Murder?" Shock made my blood run cold. "That can't be right. Why?"

She eyed me steadily. "Because of the incident at your work."

I frowned. "But he did it to protect me."

"He could have subdued the man. He chose not to."

God, she was right. I knew that. But at the time, with that gun digging painfully into my temple, I hadn't cared what Jorik had done. Now, I was glad the robber was dead. It helped me sleep at night, to work by myself in the store.

"But that's not fair."

She gave a slight shrug but said nothing.

Poor Jorik. He wasn't here. He wasn't on Earth. No wonder I'd felt so alone. He was gone. Really gone.

I licked my lips. "Can I... can I send him a message?"

She gave me a small smile, but it was the look in her eyes that had me biting my lip, made my stomach clench. "I'm so sorry, but that's not possible. Warlord Jorik was listed as missing in action twenty-six days ago after a battle with the Hive."

MIA? I knew that phrase. Missing? Still, I couldn't give up all hope. He couldn't be gone. "What does that mean? Where is he?" I whispered, barely able to get the words out.

"He was captured by the Hive, dear."

My hand flew to my mouth. I wasn't sure if I were going to be sick. Captured? The Hive? Tears filled my eyes.

"But... but he was just here. How can he be... there?"

"Jorik transported in seconds to Sector 437 and went directly to a fighting squadron."

I swallowed, licked my lips again, wiped the tears that slid down my cheeks. The warden handed me a tissue.

"Are they trying to rescue him?" I asked. It was hard to imagine someone as large and ruthless as Jorik could be captured and held against his will by anyone. I'd heard of the Hive, everyone on Earth had, but I was just like everyone else.

They were the monster under the bed, the ghost in the closet. They weren't *real*. Until now. Until the man I loved was being held prisoner. For twenty-six days.

She cocked her head to the side and reached across the desk. I slid forward, eager to accept the small comfort she offered. There was something about her that made me trust her. "There is no easy way to say this, Gabriela. The Hive integrate captured Coalition fighters. Over time, the Hive integrations steal their mind, their will, until only their body remains, and they become Hive fighters. Atlans, though, are different. As you saw during the robbery, they have an inner beast, a strength in them that is very powerful. They can withstand the Hive integrations—"

I leaned forward. "Then there's hope for him!"

"The opposite, actually. Atlans fight the integrations. Their beasts fight." She squeezed my hand and her next words stole my breath. "They fight to the death,

I'm afraid. If the Hive are patient, or determined, they will keep the Atlan alive longer, keep trying to control their beast. But most Atlans, they eliminate. An Atlan in full beast mode is a very dangerous prisoner."

I dropped back into the chair, stunned, but the tears wouldn't stop. "You're saying Jorik is dead?"

She gave me a look with a touch of pity. "His status is Captured. But it's been over three weeks. Most rescues occur within the first few days. After that...the odds—" Her voice went soft at the end and she shrugged. "I'm so sorry."

Tears fell continuously now, my hopes gone. Jorik was most likely dead. Gone.

Using the tissue, I wiped my face, then stood again. I couldn't sit here and sob. I could do that later. He had loved me. He cared. That time we spent together hadn't been my imagination. He had been mine. And now he was gone. I had all the time in the world to mourn Jorik, of what we could have had together.

But not now. I had a job to get to. Money to earn because I was having a baby. Jorik's baby. The only thing left of him.

"I'm sure he would have been pleased to know you came by to thank him. Will you be all right?" she asked, coming around the desk.

I didn't answer, for she didn't know the depth of what he meant to me.

Or perhaps, she did.

"There are many Atlan warriors out there, Gabriela. Good males. Honorable. Just like Jorik. If you ever wish to volunteer to be a bride, come see me."

I looked to her, nodded. The idea of being matched to some random Atlan held no interest. Warden Egara didn't know that, didn't know my heart belonged to Jorik, and that was why she'd made the suggestion.

"Thank you, Warden. You've been very kind."

She escorted me out of the building, and I walked to work with silent tears streaming down my cheeks. I let them run, unchecked, to soak the collar of my T-shirt. I'd only known Jorik a short time, our closeness forged by a few hours spent together. It shouldn't be so hard to be without him, but it was. My heart was broken. I put a hand over my still-flat belly. Jorik was with me. Part of me now. I thought of my baby—*our baby*—and made a vow.

I would never forget him.

We would never forget him.

5

arlord Jorik, 8 Months Later - Planet Latiri 4, The Labyrinth

CLINGING to the side of a rocky cliff by my fingertips, I glanced at the other three Warlords doing the same. With a nod to indicate we should all move, I did something I never thought I would do. As the Hive's new Hounds raced along the base of the rocky ravine, I hid. I crawled into the darkest recess of the highest cave and climbed deep into the black interior so even the Hive's drone scanners wouldn't be able to find me. I knew the other Warlords had done the same.

They were strangers to me, brothers who had been kept in cells separate from mine. I knew them only by their screams. But they fought. I knew they resisted the Hive with every breath in their bodies. They were warriors, and when I broke free and destroyed the entire Hive Integration lab, they'd been right next to me, rending and smashing and bellowing in combined rage.

Now we were free, running. Hiding. Survival drove us all. But I had one goal. One purpose in fighting for my life—getting back to my mate. To Gabriela.

I'd lost count of the days since I'd touched her soft skin, buried my cock inside her wet heat. Heard my name on her lips. Kissed her... I didn't know if the Hive had held me for two months or twenty. All I knew was I had to keep fighting. For her.

The ravine system we'd chosen for our

last stand was well-known for having magnetized rock, rock which interfered with communications on both sides of the war. The Warlords called this area The Labyrinth, and most of the Coalition Fleet's battles with the Hive on this planet were fought here. Anyone lost in these ravines was on their own and had no choice but to try to make it to one of the Coalition's beacons for any kind of rescue. If a warrior didn't activate the specially placed transmitters like we'd done, there would be no tracking by ReCon units. No comms. No extraction. No help. Right now, we were alone. We just had to wait for someone to come, to save us.

I knew that. We all did. My body, half starved for weeks and forced to consume microscopic Hive integration cells as my only source of nourishment, knew that as well.

On the surface, I looked much as I had before. But the Hive had not simply fed my body their nanotech, they'd made me strong. Abnormal. Even for an Atlan. I could crush boulders with my bare hands.

I could survive weeks without food.

I could breathe the toxic air on this planet, not for a few hours, as most of my brethren could, but indefinitely.

They'd captured a beast and made me a monster. I could never undo what they'd done to me. But I didn't care. I was still Warlord Jorik of Atlan. My mind was my own, thank the gods. And this body they'd made for me? It was mine now, too.

No, not mine. Gabriela's. Everything I had and everything I was, belonged to her. If I was stronger, I would be better able to protect her. I could use the strength to survive and get back to her.

My beast growled in agreement. He'd taken the brunt of the Hive torture. He'd fought and raged and left me alone in my mind to ignore the pain. He deserved the soft touch of our mate even more than I did, and we would make our way back to her, or die trying. There was no life worth living without her.

As for the Hive? Mind and body, I fought them. We all did. And when they missed a single dose of the chemical cocktail they had been using to keep me dazed, tamed... I'd destroyed two dozen of them. I'd hunted their lead scientist, a high-ranking Integration Unit. I'd saved that sadistic bastard for last, ripped him into pieces and left the bloody remains scattered in the cages where myself and the other Atlans had been held.

It was a warning. I wasn't sure the Hive were capable of understanding my gruesome message, but I sent it just the same.

Don't fuck with Atlans.

Just like I had on Earth and that fucker who'd had a gun to Gabriela's head. I'd told the humans the same thing. Don't fuck with Atlans.

And now there were four of us, stronger than before—thanks to their Hive integrations—waiting for a ReCon team from Battleship Karter insane enough to land in the center of The Labyrinth and save us. We'd activated the emergency beacon twelve hours ago. Twelve fucking hours.

A shift in the shadows at my cave's entrance alerted me to the presence of another of my brothers, and I held my position silently as he made his way toward me. When we were both facing out where we could watch for an attack, Wulf spoke for the first time in hours.

"The Hounds have moved on," he murmured.

"They'll be back."

He sighed and I waited for the bad news.

"I've fought on the Karter for years. It takes about eight hours to muster a ReCon team and get them down here."

I knew where he was going with this, but I refused to give up. Not yet. "What's your point, Commander?"

"They're not coming, Jorik," he replied, his voice devoid of all emotion. Not that he ever showed any. "They're already four hours late. We have to go back to the Integration Center and steal a Hive shuttle."

My head was shaking before I'd even formed a thought. "No. The place was already swarming with hundreds of them when we got out. More arriving by transport every few minutes because of what we did. There could be a thousand Hive soldiers there now, guarding those shuttles."

"I know. But we'll take as many of them down as we can." Wulf's words held a finality I refused to accept.

"Even if we can get one, the Karter will blast us into a thousand pieces before we get close to the battleship."

He sighed, knowing the truth of my words. "We'll worry about that after we steal the shuttle."

"No. We wait."

"I'm the Commander, Jorik. If I tell the others to move out, they will."

"And you'd all still be rotting in those cells if it weren't for me," I countered. "I have a mate, Commander. I need to get back to her. Give me a few more hours, at least." Turning my head, I looked Wulf in the eyes so he knew I meant what I said. I couldn't give up so easily. "Two hours. If they don't show, I'll destroy the entire fucking planet to get back to her."

Wulf grinned, the first sign of hope I'd seen in months, and slapped me on the back hard enough to bruise. I didn't care. Pain meant I was still alive. "Agreed. Two more hours. Then we attack."

Thank the gods. "What about the others?"

Wulf said what I expected, but I still needed to hear it. "They'll wait for my orders."

We waited in silence and I had to admit, I was glad for the company. Thirty minutes passed. An hour. Two.

I knew precisely what time it was, every cell in my body knew, thanks to the Hive. I felt the passing of every moment as if hope left my body drop by drop with each second that passed. I strained to listen for the sounds of approaching warriors, engines, anything that would indicate they were coming.

Silence.

"Two hours, Jorik. I'm sorry," Wulf said simply.

"I know." I didn't want to agree, but he'd compromised, and so would I.

We crawled forward and looked out over the ravine. There was no sign of the Hive Scouts or their Hounds, but I wasn't fooled. They wouldn't be far, and those Hounds could move faster than most planets' EVs.

Wulf hung onto the edge, looking over. He whistled softly and two more Atlans appeared as if they'd melted into the rocks and now reemerged to form a solid shape.

With one point of Wulf's finger, the others crawled up toward the top of the cliffs to claim high ground. The Integration Center was buried deep inside a cave about two miles from our current position. Undetectable by Coalition scanners, we had no idea how long the Hive stronghold had been there, their close proximity made it all too easy for them to scavenge the wounded from the battlefield and take them directly into an Integration Unit. Right under Commander Karter's fucking nose.

It was genius. And so very fucking practical. So very Hive.

No wonder they never quite gave up control of this planet. To them, it was a fucking Hive factory. So many warriors. So many battles. Countless Coalition lives lost. All so the Hive could feed their insatiable need to consume other races.

"Let's go," Wulf ordered. "We stay low and move fast. Keep your beast under control until he's needed."

"Understood." I would have scoffed at his final order if it hadn't been my beast who'd spoken to him last. *I know.* Two words that caused me too much pain to speak. So he'd spoken for both of us. Now I had to get my beast under control, take back the burden of the pain so we could move, quietly. Quickly. Sneak in like shadows and turn our monsters free. We wouldn't survive. There was no fucking way we would ever reach those shuttles. We all knew the truth. But we'd take out as many of the bastards as we could as we died.

It beat hiding in a cave and waiting... for nothing. Losing hope.

We'd run half the distance when Wulf came to an abrupt stop, lifting his arm as a signal for us to cease moving.

Once my heartbeat settled and was no longer pounding in my ears, I heard what he'd heard.

A shuttle engine. Coming from the opposite direction of the Hive's stronghold.

My beast howled, as if summoning the shuttle to us.

Two minutes later, it landed on the rugged terrain, and I was staring down into the face of a small human ReCon captain.

Wulf bellowed and pulled the smaller man into a fierce, bone crushing hug.

"Fuck, Wulf, it's good to see you. Easy

on the ribs. We gotta get the hell out of here." The captain and his team surrounded us, armed to the teeth. I didn't bother to take one of their ion rifles. I didn't need one to fight. Not anymore.

"Seth. Fuck. I thought you weren't coming." Wulf let him go, then stepped back and slapped him on the shoulder. "You're a fucking idiot for coming, you know that?"

The captain laughed. "Oh, I know. Stupid ass job. And if I don't get my ass off this rock alive, Chloe's going to beat me to death."

Wulf laughed and, as if some magical signal had been passed between the two males, they turned in unison and ran back to the waiting shuttle. The rest of us fell into line and my heart pounded harder than it had since the escape. Not with fear, with anticipation. Need.

Gabriela.

The shuttle door closed behind us and I reached for the captain, but Wulf beat me to him as we lifted off the ground, the metal floor shifting beneath our feet.

"Hold on back there!" The ReCon team, except for Seth, had buckled back in to their seats. But the ReCon shuttles were not made to hold a beast, and we braced the best we could in the small cargo area. Beside me, Kai and Egon held on, neither speaking. Leaving that up to their commander.

"Seth, I need to speak to Karter," Wulf said.

Seth nodded. "No problem. I'll set up a comm as soon as we clear the atmosphere."

Wulf looked grim, as did the two Atlans standing on either side of me. "And Commander Phan."

That made Seth's smile fade. "Commander Phan?" I didn't understand until he asked his next question. "Not Chloe?"

"Yes. And any other Intelligence Core officers on the Karter."

"That bad?" Seth asked, his voice grim. "I don't want my mate dragged into anything else. She's already doing more than I would like. It's fucking dangerous, Wulf."

"It's worse than any of us imagined," Kai, the blond Atlan on my right confirmed what we'd all been thinking. "The Hive have what is basically a body farm, a factory for the dying and wounded to be taken and assimilated, right here on Latiri 4. Right under the battlegroup's fucking nose."

Seth remained silent as we cleared the atmosphere with little turbulence and I slumped in relief as the ship's nominal gravity kicked in. We were safe. We were saved. All at once, I was tired. My beast was tired. Even that small respite felt good. Not as good as sinking into Gabriela's warm body would feel, but damn good all the same.

Wulf fell into step behind Seth as they made their way toward the cockpit. I followed behind. Seth was human. He would know how to contact Earth. How to find my female.

But duty came first, and I allowed Wulf to make his call to the frightening Prillon commander named Karter. I'd never met him, but the way the crew responded to his every word let me know he was respected. Wulf spoke to him with great respect, and that was enough for me.

When Wulf had passed along the coordinates and basic details, they set a time for a full debriefing. I would be required to be there, and I couldn't argue with that either. I knew that facility inside out. I'd seen most of it. Counted the number of occupants, their transport schedule, everything I thought might be useful, I'd made note of. The others had done the same.

But then, the call was over and my beast would not wait another moment. He burst free, my face elongating, my body growing until I had to bend at the waist to stand in the small shuttle.

"Seth." My beast's deep rumble brought all conversation to an abrupt halt.

"Yes, Warlord?" Seth tilted his head

and stared at me, not at all frightened. He was either an idiot, or one of the bravest men I'd ever met.

"Comm Earth. Mate. Gabriela."

Seth grinned at me. Fucker. "Earth's a big place, friend."

My beast, tortured, ravaged, half starved—he didn't much care for the captain's answer. Before I could process the movement, Seth's neck was in my hand, his body dangling off the floor. The low gravity kept me from strangling him, but would not prevent me from crushing his neck, popping his spine from his body like popping a cork from a bottle of wine. "Miami."

Wulf's hand came to rest on my shoulder. He didn't attack. He knew better. My beast was not feeling particularly reasonable at the moment. And fuck all, I wasn't either. Not after all this time. I couldn't wait a second longer.

"Captain," Wulf spoke. "You'd best make a comm to Earth. You don't want to fuck with coming between a beast and his mate."

The human lifted his brows. "Put me down, Warlord. We'll call your mate," he replied, the simple words soothing me.

My beast grunted in distrust but set the smaller human down on his feet. One wrong move, and I wasn't even going to try to stop the beast from making my point crystal clear. My mate was on Earth. Alone. Unprotected.

Mine.

Seth turned to the pilot and nodded his head. Next thing we all heard was a woman's voice coming through the comm system. "This is CFPC-Earth. How may I assist you?"

CFPC. Coalition Fleet Processing Center. Brides and fighters.

I didn't care about warriors coming from that planet. Or brides. There was only one female I cared about.

"This is Captain Seth Mills of Battlegroup Karter, Sector 437. I need to locate a human female immediately. Her mate has just been rescued from a Hive Integration Center. His mate should be notified at once."

"Wonderful!" The woman's voice through the shuttle's comm system sounded genuinely pleased, and my beast settled more. There was no stress in the female's voice. No worry. Perhaps, like this female, my mate was well. Safe. Relaxed and secure. "What is the woman's name?"

Seth looked at me, and thankfully, I was back to normal size, so I could speak. "Gabriela Olivas Silva." I gave the woman Gabriela's address as well, memorized and held as precious information during my captivity.

"Hold, please."

The line went silent, but not dead, and everyone on board the shuttle waited anxiously. Some with curiosity, me with urgent need. A few moments later, the woman spoke again.

"I'm sorry, Captain, there is no bride registered under that name."

Seth looked to me.

I pushed the beast back enough so I could speak clearly. "She's not a bride. I met her on Earth. She lives near the processing center."

"I see." Was that disapproval in the female's voice? "I will have to contact her directly then, using local means. What is her mate's name?"

Wulf answered. "Warlord Jorik of Atlan."

There was a startled gasp, cut off by silence. Then the female's voice once more. "Please hold once more. I will make contact with the female."

Several more minutes passed. Each second felt like an hour. And when the female's voice returned, I wished it hadn't.

"I'm so sorry, Captain Mills," the woman finally said. "I have located the woman. She came to the center, looking for her mate after he was removed from service here. He had been captured and was presumed dead and she was told as much. I'm afraid she moved on and married someone else. A human."

"What?" *What? Married?* That was a human word, but my NPU was telling me what I didn't want to know. "She has a new mate?"

"I'm sorry, Warlord," the female replied. "She thought you were dead. She got married three months ago." Her voice was full of pity, as were the looks of every member of the ReCon team, the Atlans, and Wulf. *Fuck. Fuck. Fuck.*

Uninvited, the feminine voice continued. "I don't see you in the system, Warlord. I assume that as a warrior rescued from the Hive, you will be transferred to The Colony. I'm advising you that you now will qualify for an Interstellar Bride as you survived your capture. You should submit for processing as soon as you arrive on The Colony."

Get tested for a bride? No fucking way. If I couldn't have Gabriela, no one else would do. My beast would not consider another, and neither would I.

I couldn't speak, so the captain did it for me. His shoulders slumped and his eyes grew dark, as if he understood my pain. "Thank you, ma'am. Captain Mills out."

The line went silent, but I paid no attention. I sank to the shuttle floor and laid on my back, staring at nothing. Dead inside, my beast, for the first time, was completely silent.

6

J orik, Fighting Pits, The Colony

THE TWO PRILLON warriors I'd been fighting didn't come back for more. The first, was unconscious where I'd thrown him into the wall. The second clawed at the dirt as he attempted to regain his footing, blood dripping from his head to soak the reddish ground.

"Down!" My beast bellowed at the idiot for trying to stand. He should stay down, not challenge the raging monster fully on display. Not just my beast, but what the Hive had made me. We'd lost our mate. Pain was our constant existence, and I took it out here. In the pit. It was the only sanctioned place to fight on this planet.

As usual, the beast took over, bore the brunt of my rage, but was much more difficult to control. Especially here in the pits.

Even the normally roaring crowd of observers was oddly silent, and I heard footsteps behind me. Turned to find Wulf, Kai, Egon, Braun, and Tane walking forward to encircle me. They gave me space, plenty of it, but I was surrounded.

Five against one? And all Atlans.

My beast smiled. There would be no holding back. No restraint.

I roared, but the others did not respond as I anticipated, and my beast raised his arms, "Come. Fight."

"No," Wulf spoke, shaking his head, but the Warlord Braun, beside him, was in full beast form. The others, all but Wulf, were in the process of changing to their beasts as well. Quietly. All five of them. "We are here to take you down, Jorik."

"Fight." I did not like what I was hearing, and my beast liked it even less. We needed more. More pain. More blood. More. It was the only way I could feel, the only outlet to my anguish. My rage.

"No more fighting," Wulf continued. "You've been out of control since your arrival. The governor has ordered us to take care of it."

"Fight."

"You're coming with us, Jorik, or you're going to Bundar Prison."

So, they thought I'd lost control, needed to be executed. Five fellow Atlans all agreed I was too far gone.

Perhaps they were right. I found no light in the world. No hope.

No Gabriela.

Yet, even as the male part of me grieved, my beast refused to go down without a fight. For nearly a year he'd fought to escape the Hive. He was strong, stronger than I was, and he simply refused to die. He also refused to give up the hope that someday Gabriela would be ours.

"NO!"

I—we—my beast charged at Wulf but was caught around the neck by Braun and slammed onto my back mid-stride. Immediately, the others fell on me, holding me down. Restraining me, but not hurting me. The contaminated monster I'd been turned into could try to take them, but somehow, I knew, I didn't want to harm any of them.

And yet, it was unacceptable. I needed the pain. The release.

"Fight!" I bellowed, struggling with every ounce of enhanced cyborg strength I possessed, but the others were contaminated as well. Stronger than a normal Atlan. Harder in mind and body. They held me as I thrashed and raged, my roars changing to screams.

"You nearly killed those two Prillons, Jorik," Wulf growled. "But I'm just as stubborn as you are. I know you're upset about the female, but I'm not letting you die. Not after every fucking thing we went through." Wulf squatted next to my head as the others held me. My rage had turned to tears, and still I fought for my freedom.

So I could hurt. So I could kill.

So I could die.

"No," I snapped.

"You will come with us," Wulf continued. "You will sit your ass down in the Bride Program testing chair, and you'll be matched to a female worthy of you. Do you hear me, Warlord? That's an order."

I gritted my teeth, tried to roll out from under the four other beasts holding me down. All I managed was to scrape a good portion of skin off my back on the rocks and gravel lining the fighting pit. Even the scent of my own blood did not calm me, but the beast didn't want to fight his friends, those who'd suffered with us at the hands of the enemy. My beast retreated, leaving me to face Wulf alone. Just a male. Weak.

"Just send me to Bundar Prison, Wulf," I said, finally done. "I'm too far gone."

"I will not lose you, and not to a containment facility like that," he countered. "Not over a female who was not your mate."

"She's mine," I snapped.

"She's not. Gabriela thought you were dead, Jorik. We were in that hell for nearly a year. She has another mate. She's happy. Protected. Cared for. Do you wish to destroy her happiness? Break her heart? Hurt her?"

"Never."

Wulf stood, the light of the star shining off his hair like some kind of celestial being's as he spoke to the others. "Drag his ass to the testing chair. Make sure he completes the process. Don't leave his side until the doctor says it's complete."

The others hauled me to my feet, and I felt like a child walking among them. I was surrounded, guided. There would be no escaping my fate. But I didn't care.

Didn't care about anything. But Wulf was right. Gabriela had moved on. She was lost to me. Fate had been a fucking bitch and taken her from me. Now it was too late.

I would never hurt her. Never ask her to choose between myself and another worthy male, a male who loved her. A male who'd been there for her when I couldn't be.

My shoulders slumped in defeat, and I spit the metallic taste of blood from my mouth as we cleared the pits and headed toward the medical station.

So be it.

A large hand came to rest on my shoulder.

Braun.

"You will survive this, brother," he said, as if it were another painful Hive torture session.

I didn't reply. I didn't much care one way or another. There were several thousand warriors on The Colony. While many had been tested, only a handful had been matched. The odds were slim that any female would be matched to me, especially since my beast and I both knew Gabriela was the only female for me. But my cooperation would appease Wulf, and the governor. Because despite what my broken heart demanded, I was too fucking stubborn to die.

7

*G*abriela, Earth

I SHOULD NAP. God, my eyelids felt like they were coated with sand. Jori was sound asleep in his car seat I'd set down by the front door, and I had about an hour until he would wake up hungry. Again. Although he hadn't quite gotten the hang of a schedule yet. I glanced at the couch longingly. I could tip over onto the soft cushions and close my eyes. Oh, the bliss.

But first I had to put the groceries away or they'd spoil, then shower, perhaps do a load of laundry. The sweats I wore, although ratty, were my last clean pair, and I doubted they would survive the day.

Babies—at least my baby—were messy creatures.

Beautiful, miraculous, messy creatures.

I grabbed the two bags and carried them into the kitchen, put the eggs in the fridge. I winced, feeling the pull of the incision. I shouldn't have carried the car seat and the grocery bags from the car, but I'd had no choice. I wouldn't leave Jori alone, either in the car or inside while I moved the bags. And now I would need another pain pill. I wasn't supposed to drive, but I needed to eat.

I turned, saw my reflection in the microwave. Wished I hadn't.

My hair was up in a sloppy bun, I had no makeup on. My tank top did nothing to hide my new curves... and I had plenty. Penthouse centerfolds had nothing on my new mommy boobs. I'd barely left the house since I got home from the hospital, and when I did, I didn't primp, let alone get fancied up. I could barely get both of us dressed and out the door before Jori pooped himself and needed a whole new outfit. How did something so little get poop everywhere?

And then there was my incision, the bandages, the constant bleeding.

Ugh. I had no idea having a baby was so... messy.

From the other room, I heard a little snuffle. Going around the counter, I peeked down at my son.

Or so very worth it.

God, I loved him already. So much. His nose scrunched up and his hands clenched into fists as he slept. In his little blue onesie with the words Mama's Boy on the chest, every roll of perfect baby fat was visible. Tubby thighs and dimpled elbows, every inch of him was perfect. And big. It was amazing he was eight days old.

It had gone by in a blur, and yet so impossibly slow.

I had no family to help out, only a few friends, but they either had families of their own or worked. I was sleep deprived; I couldn't remember the last time I showered, and even then, if I'd actually put shampoo in my hair—or remembered to rinse it out. All the books told me this was normal, that I was normal, but I was going to have to go back to work in a few weeks. I would have to shower. Dress in clothes that were clean. Sleep more than two hours at a time. Be able to stand upright without wincing from being cut open to have a huge-ass baby pulled out of me. Be able to put two thoughts together, because God, where did my brain go?

Jori stuck his little legs out and let out a wail. The little man had some serious lungs. I glanced at the clock on the stove, thought it was a too early for him to be hungry again, but it wasn't for me to decide. If he was hungry, he let it be known.

After undoing the straps on the car

seat, I picked him up and snuggled him close, kissed his soft head, laughed when his fist bopped me in the cheek.

"All right, you can have a snack," I told him, carefully settling onto the couch in the corner where I could get in the best position to nurse. Lifting my tank top, I opened the flap on my nursing bra and settled him into a football hold. He knew where he was going and latched on easily. Smart little man.

"You're just like your father," I told him, exploding with emotions. "A boob man." The whispered words made me giggle, not because they were that funny, but because I was three quarters delirious, missing Jorik, mourning him all over again every time I looked at Jori's dark hair and eyes, and trying to hold back the terrifying thought that I was solely responsible for another life. I was a mother.

And all I could do to honor and remember my one love was to name his son after him.

Tears rolled as Jori made a sweet

sound, his tiny fist wrapping around my fingertip as his little mouth sucked. My son. Jorik's son. I loved him so much it hurt. Actually hurt. The moment was bittersweet, and lonely, and I wasn't sure I was going to survive this alone.

But the gorgeous boy was completely unaware of my mixed-up emotions. He didn't respond, just sucked away as if he hadn't eaten two hours earlier, and two hours before that. My nipples were sore, my body ached like I'd been hit by a truck —not delivered a baby—and the cut from the C-section made holding him across my lap extremely painful.

And it was perfect.

I settled back, closed my eyes. Sighed and let my thoughts go where they usually did. To Jorik. The way he'd looked at me, with a mix of curiosity and possession. I remembered everything about him. His dark hair, strong hands. Muscled torso. Big cock. Strong legs. I'd had nine months to relive every one of my memories. Again and again.

Memories were all I had of him, besides Jori. I was fiercely protective of our
baby. I hadn't told Warden Egara I was
pregnant, didn't let anyone know anything
about my connection to Jorik. At first, it
seemed as if I were shaming Jorik's
memory by lying, telling the doctors that
Jori had been conceived during a random
hookup from one of those online dating
sites. But I'd quickly realized I wasn't just
having Jorik's baby, I was having an Atlan
baby. An alien.

There were no alien babies on Earth.
There were barely any adult aliens, and
they were confined, watched. Just like
Jorik had been. Sent away to fight in the
war with the Hive at the slightest indiscre-
tion. Okay, ripping someone's head off
wasn't very slight, but he'd been protecting me.

God, I wondered where he would be
right now if it hadn't been for me. He
wouldn't have killed that guy—not that I
was complaining—and wouldn't have

been banished. Sent to fight the Hive. Captured.

What ifs. But if I hadn't met him, I wouldn't have Jori, and I couldn't imagine that. I couldn't find it in myself to regret any of it. And that was why I was so careful now, so cautious with my son. He didn't look Atlan, other than the fact that he was big. Really big for a baby, but otherwise any alien-ness wasn't noticeable.

I told the doctor his father was a football player, a professional. The biggest human males I could think of at the time. He'd believed me, and even made a comment about my *"new little linebacker"* in the operating room once he'd pulled him from me and lifted him above the sheet they'd put up so I couldn't see them cutting me open. The lie seemed to be working, at least for now. I just had to hope no one would ever know, for if they'd taken Jorik away, I wondered if they'd take Jori away, too.

And that was not happening. Anyone tried to take my son and they'd discover

Atlans weren't the only ones with an inner beast.

Jorik had protected me, and I would honor him by raising his son to be just like him. Caring. Protective. Honorable.

"It's you and me, kid," I murmured, shifting him to my shoulder to pat his back. It didn't take him long to burp, then I switched him to the other side. Thankfully, we'd gotten the hang of nursing right away.

I missed Jorik, longed for him, but accepted that he wasn't coming back. For months I clung to hope that I'd see him again, but that was slowly fading. It had been hard when I was pregnant, when I gave birth without him. I wished he could have shared those experiences with me, and now, too, watching Jori grow bigger by the day.

I must have fallen asleep because pounding on the door startled me. Jori was still on my boob, but no longer nursing. He, too, was asleep.

I blinked and someone knocked again. God, I had both boobs out!

"Just a minute," I called, then shifted Jori onto the couch beside me so I could fix my clothes.

Picking him up, I patted his little butt, then answered the door.

Before me were two men in uniforms identical to what Jorik had worn. My heart leapt into my throat at the familiar outfit.

"Yes?"

"Gabriela Silva?" The one on the left asked, then glanced down at Jori who was tucked in my arm.

"Yes," I said again, this time with a little wariness in my voice.

"Ma'am, your presence has been requested at the Coalition Fleet Processing Center."

My gut was telling me they were trouble. Not trouble like the robber at the ice cream store, for I didn't feel in danger. I felt like... like, God, I had no idea.

"Did they find Jorik?" I asked, trying to

glance around them to see if he might be behind. As if he wouldn't have knocked them down to get to me. Or at least that was what I'd dreamed he'd do.

The one on the right frowned. "We don't know this person, Jorik. Please come with us."

"I need to leave the baby with Mrs. Taylor down the hall."

They shook their heads in unison. "Ma'am, that's not possible. The request is for both you and the baby."

Oh god, I'd been right. They'd found out about Jori and were going to take him away. Send him to some family in Atlan.

No way. I wouldn't let them have my baby.

"No," I told them. "Get near my child and I'll rip your heads off."

"Ma'am," one of them said again, but I wasn't paying attention to who. They held up their hands in front of them. "You can hold your baby."

I stepped back, tried to push the door

closed, but one of them put their foot in the way.

"Ma'am."

"Stop ma'am'ing me!" I shouted. Jori startled and started to cry. I started to cry. "You can't take my baby!"

I heard voices as I leaned my shoulder into the door, trying to keep them out, but over Jori's cries and my heart pounding in my ears, I could barely make them out. The foot remained between the hard wood and the frame, but no one was pushing me back. They were bigger than me—not Atlan sized—but could easily overpower me. "Yes. Upset. Yes. No, I don't want to make a scene. Yes. We'll wait."

I turned and leaned my back against the door, trying to close it as I patted Jori's back, shushing him. I breathed him in, his sweet, baby scent as I held him close. I wouldn't let them take him.

"Gabriela."

I heard my name, this time from a woman.

"Gabriela, this is Warden Egara from

the Interstellar Brides Processing Center. We met a number of months ago. I apologize for scaring you by sending the guards. They were following my orders to bring you in."

I didn't move, didn't do anything but methodically pat Jori's back and continue to lean against the door.

"Can you let the captain have his foot back?" she asked.

"I won't let you take my baby!" I cried.

"Of course not," she countered. "I put families together. I do not tear them apart. And I would *never* take a child from a mother who loves him."

"How do I know you're not tricking me?" That *never* she'd said sounded like she'd taken offense at the mere suggestion. Still, this was my *son* we were talking about. I was taking no chances.

"Because while he is Atlan, he is also human, and he needs his mother."

My hand stilled, my heart leapt into my throat. She knew. Holy shit. *She knew.*

I stepped away from the door and it

opened slowly. Warden Egara entered, then closed it behind her, leaving the guards outside.

"He's beautiful," she said, smiling at Jori who was already back asleep. Adorable. "What's his name?"

"Jori, but I think you knew that."

She looked exactly as I'd met her months ago when she'd help me get information about Jorik. Sleek bun, crisp uniform.

"It isn't very often a fourteen-pound baby is born," she said.

Jori had been huge, so big that they'd thought my due date had been miscalculated. There had been no way I was pushing a bowling ball out, so they'd recommended a planned C-section a week before my due date, which I'd gladly agreed upon. There had been nothing noteworthy about the birth—thank god— except he was big.

"You saw the article about him?" A stupid nurse at the hospital had told his wife about the baby, and *she* was a journalist for a local TV station. One thing led to another, and the next thing I knew, there were reporters in front of the hospital when we left, Jori's feet already hanging over the edge of the new car seat. He wasn't just heavy, he was long. I had no idea how he'd even fit inside my body, poor scrunched up little guy.

Sidetracked. Jeez. I tore my gaze from my son to find Warden Egara watching me closely.

She nodded. "I did. But not until today. I was on vacation, and it didn't come up in my feed search until now. You wanted to find Warlord Jorik that day, but not just to thank him."

She didn't state it as a question. I shook my head. "No. I loved him. I wanted him to know I was pregnant. But it doesn't matter now. He's gone."

"It does matter." She tipped her chin toward Jori, who was now asleep. "Your son is half Atlan. He can't remain here on Earth."

I took a step back. "You're not taking

him from me. Like I told the guards, I'll rip you to pieces if you touch him."

She laughed. "Yes, I believe you would. I wouldn't dare take him from you. But you will have to leave Earth behind. Your son may look human now, but he will not be a normal boy growing up. He will not be happy here."

"Where am I supposed to go?" My head spun and panic threatened to choke me. Where was I supposed to go? An alien planet? To Atlan? How would I live? I didn't know anyone or anything about another state, let alone another planet. I didn't want another mate. I had a plan, a job, an apartment. I could raise a baby on my own, here. At home. On Earth.

Her huge smile confused me even more. "I don't often have the chance to do this. That is why I wished to do it in person."

"Do what?"

"I have the good news of telling you that Warlord Jorik has escaped the Hive.

He is alive and well and has been transferred to The Colony."

My heart practically leapt into my throat at her words. "Wha... what?"

Her smile was lovely. I thought that as my legs gave out, and I lowered myself to a chair. "Jorik's alive?"

"Yes, and because you have an Atlan child, *his* child, I can send you to him without the usual red tape. It is Earth law that no aliens are allowed in the general population. Coalition law states that families must be together. Therefore, you and your son are going to The Colony to live with Warlord Jorik."

I licked my lips. Blinked. Was this possible? Could it be true? Had my dreams, my desires to be with Jorik again, that he wasn't actually captured and killed, come true?

"That is what you want, isn't it?"

What was this Colony like? What did that even mean?

Did it matter?

No. It didn't. I had no one here, no one but Jori. And he needed his father.

I needed his father.

I nodded. "Yes, that is what I want above anything else. When?"

"I must process you, give you an NPU and the regulatory implants required to live among other member of the Fleet, but you'll be with Jorik now, Gabriela. Today."

8

J orik, Transport Room 4, The Colony

I COULDN'T BELIEVE IT. I *wouldn't* believe it. Not until she was here. Gabriela was coming to The Colony. Now.

I stood at the base of the transport platform, legs wide, hands at my sides but clenched in fists. There was me, the transport tech, Governor Rone and we stared at... nothing. The platform was empty. We waited. And waited. The room was silent.

I'd waited countless days... weeks,

months, to see Gabriela again, dreamed of her, relived every moment, every look, every touch, and I could barely hold it together. While I didn't feel like ripping anyone's head off any longer, my beast was practically clawing at me with impatience. I spun on my heel and glared at the transport tech.

"Where the fuck is she?" He stared at me wide-eyed from behind the control podium, but since he, too, was integrated like everyone on this planet, he'd been through hell and back. A snapping Atlan didn't scare him. "Why aren't you doing something?"

"Because there is nothing to do," he replied evenly. "The transport was arranged and initiated by Earth."

I turned back around, stared some more at the metal floor of the pad where Gabriela would arrive.

"Easy, Warlord. She is coming."

I looked to the governor, who stood beside me, and narrowed my eyes. "You can't be sure."

Nodding his head, he said, "I can. I spoke to Warden Egara personally."

I knew who Warden Egara was, so I had some idea how trustworthy this human could be. He crossed his arms over his broad chest and stared at the transport pad. Obviously, he trusted her as well.

"I spoke to someone on Earth before and she told me Gabriela married a male from Earth, that she'd chosen a new mate," I told him, although he already knew that.

"That must have been a mistake, Jorik."

My beast was impatient, growing angry as I thought of the last few days, of the pain and torment I'd gone through. "You *forced* me to be tested for a new bride."

He shrugged, unconcerned he'd been wrong. "Well, you weren't matched. And you *were* on the verge of killing my warriors in the fighting pit."

I frowned, not needing the reminder of

my loss of control. I reined in my beast, forced myself to calm. Gabriela was coming. To me. She was mine. She'd agreed. "So Gabriela did not choose another mate?"

"No. Warden Egara said they must have looked up the wrong woman. A mistake, nothing more."

A *mistake* that nearly drove me mad and almost cost two good warriors their lives in the pits.

The vibrations beneath my feet cut off my thoughts. I had no interest in talking now that the first sign of an incoming transport had begun. I whipped my gaze off the governor and onto the pad. The hairs on my body stood on end, and I felt the familiar sizzle of transport.

"Incoming," the tech said, although more out of protocol to warn everyone to remain away from the transport pad than to state the obvious.

Between one blink and the next, there she was, lying on her back, asleep. I dashed up the steps, knelt before her.

I glanced up at the governor, then back at the unconscious form of Gabriela.

She was here. But she was not alone. She held, snug to her chest, a baby.

I took in so many things at once, I was confused. It was she, the same dark hair, the beautiful face I remember so clearly, but she did not look well. Her skin was pale, the area around her eyes sunken with exhaustion and dark circles. She was covered in soft pants and a large shirt, but her breasts were much larger, her soft, rounded stomach even more so.

So soft. I couldn't wait to explore every single change in my mate's body. Relearn her. Worship her.

But... *there was a baby.*

It, too, was asleep, and very small. Newly born, if I had to guess. I couldn't tell if the child was a boy or a girl. The little one was wrapped in a white blanket. But its hair was as dark as Gabriela's. Black.

The little one blinked, just a bit, and I saw dark eyes staring back at me.

The baby's skin was darker than Gabriela's as well.

As dark as mine.

"She has a baby," I murmured. A baby. An infant. How? Why? What...? Who was the father? Had she been married after all? Had she chosen a new mate? What? Who had touched her? Was she still mine? Did she love another?

I couldn't work through the chaos of my thoughts, or the emotional storm of seeing her again.

"Yes. Warden Egara mentioned, Warlord, that you have a child."

I stopped breathing. My beast paused as well.

Mine? The little one was mine? All the while I'd been captured and tortured, my mate had gone through a pregnancy alone on that backward planet? With those savages for doctors?

I had a child! My beast howled.

"You didn't think to tell me?" I growled even as my hands trembled, as I reached for my mate and my baby. I lifted them into my arms, narrowing my eyes at him.

"And miss the look on your face right now?" He grinned, slapped me on the back.

The governor reached for the infant and my beast growled, practically snapped at him. He yanked his hands back. "Easy, Warlord. I wish your family no harm. I will hold the infant while you check on your mate."

The idea was sound—and he had children of his own—so I nodded, accepting his assistance, for there was no doubt my mate did need help. She looked like she had suffered. Weak. Drained. Exhausted. She'd transported through space when she was already recovering from carrying my child. I was an Atlan. She was small. Human.

And so fucking beautiful. So strong. I'd never seen anything so perfect in my life.

With gentle hands, the governor scooped up the infant and held it close to his chest. He didn't move, didn't take a step away, probably sensing my beast would attack if he did. I didn't know who to look at, who to protect, my beast instinctively screaming *mine* toward both of them.

With the baby out of the way, I studied Gabriela. "What the fuck has happened to her?"

I was the one who'd been captured by the Hive. Put through hell. Her hair, usually sleek and smooth, was pulled up atop her head in something humans called a bun. I'd seen her style her hair like this when she'd worked at the ice cream store, but it was tangled, snarled and lacked the glossy sheen I remembered. Her face lacked the usual flush, dark circles were beneath her eyes. She wore a shirt just like the one she'd worn when working at the ice cream store, but this one was several sizes too large and was wrinkled and stained. Her pants were loose and threadbare. She smelled, strange, a combination of my son's scent mingled with the feminine sweetness I remembered. But there was more. Odd. Plastic. Oil. Strangely sweet soap and soured milk, the former coming from the infant, the latter from the large stain on the shoulder of Gabriela's shirt.

"By looking at the age of the baby, I'd assume she's recently given birth," he said.

I stared at her some more, then snapped out of it, carefully cradling her in my arms and settled her in my lap. She was heavier than I remembered, her curves even more lush.

She was here, in my arms and no one, *no one,* would separate us again. My beast howled with happiness.

"Warlord. You are overwhelmed."

I looked up at him. He stood on a lower step as I sat on the hard floor, but he was still taller.

"Wouldn't you be?" I countered.

He grinned. "Absolutely. Congratulations."

"Why are they asleep?" I asked,

standing carefully. "Something is not right. Look at Gabriela. She should have regained consciousness by now. She is ill. I must get her to the medical unit immediately."

I wanted to grab the infant from his arms to hold it close and protect it with my body.

The governor must have sensed my internal conflict, for he said, "I will stay with you, I promise. I will not separate you from your infant, but you can't tend to your mate and hold the infant at the same time."

Grudgingly, I knew he was right. I appreciated his calm efficiency and clear head, for I had neither.

A few minutes later, I carefully placed Gabriela on an examination table, and a Prillon doctor began to wave a wand over her, scanning. I eyed the governor, ensured he stood a few feet away from me, but nowhere near the unit's entrance. He wasn't leaving.

Perhaps the doctor sensed I wasn't

moving from her side and did all of the assessments across from me.

As he did so, Gabriela stirred, blinked, then opened her eyes. In an instant, I leaned over her so she saw my face, nothing else. I grinned at her, stroked my knuckles down her soft cheek. God, this was the moment I'd longed for all this time. She was here, she was awake and she was *mine.*

"Mate," I breathed.

"Jorik," she whispered, staring at me almost unbelievingly. Her eyes filled with tears. "Jorik!" she shouted, even though I was right above her, and then she began to sob. Her hands came up and she wrapped her arms about my neck, as if afraid I would go somewhere. She cried, the sound the worst pain I could endure. "Are you real? Don't leave me."

Never.

"Shh," I crooned, stroking her hair, trying to soothe her. "I'm here and everything's fine."

Her body shook as she cried and

clung. I looked to the doctor who didn't look concerned, only waited with blatant patience.

Finally, her tears dried up and she hiccupped once, then loosened her hold. Her hand came to my cheek and she stared at me with those gorgeous, glistening eyes.

I couldn't wait a moment longer. I lowered my head, kissed her. Her lips were so soft, so familiar I almost wept with happiness. My cock surged with desire. My heart... my heart was full.

She startled and tried to sit up, almost hitting our heads together, before she collapsed back onto the table in obvious pain. "Oh my god. Jori! Where's Jori?" she cried.

I realized she wasn't saying my name a second time but was referring to the infant. "Shh," I said. "The baby is right here."

I moved back just enough for the governor to stand beside me so she could see the infant. Jori.

"He is well?" she asked. "The transport or whatever didn't hurt him?"

He. A son. I had a *son*.

"He is well," I told her, swallowing hard to keep my own emotions in check. She didn't need a crying Atlan right now. "Sleeping peacefully."

She relaxed again, setting a hand on her lower belly. Sighed. I was glad to put her at ease, but I did not like the lines of strain around her eyes, the glaze of pain I saw in her gaze. Tears slipped from the corners of her eyes once more.

More tears.

My beast prowled, threatened to explode from my body. My mate was in pain.

I looked at the doctor. "She is still crying. What is wrong with her?"

"Warlord, your mate is suffering from anemia, exhaustion, hormone imbalance and has extensive internal injuries," the doctor said.

My head snapped up to the Prillon warrior. "What? Explain." Was she losing blood? Was that why she was pale?

"As you're aware, she's recently given birth. It would appear the human doctors removed the child surgically. The effects of both the pregnancy and the surgical procedure are still ailing her."

"Why?" That was ridiculous. No females suffered this for a child.

"Earth is not a full member of the Coalition. They do not have access to ReGen technology. Her body has been trying to heal on its own."

"I'm fine. The NPU is giving me a headache and the other body function implants feel...odd. But I'm fine, really. Jorik, help me up," Gabriela said, her palm still resting on her lower stomach.

Putting my arm around her shoulders, I carefully helped Gabriela sit, but I didn't remove my hold.

"I'm not injured," she said. "You sound as if I went into battle. I gave birth. Last week. To an Atlan," she added, with a hint of sarcasm.

I grinned then, I couldn't help it. She was well enough to sass us, she would recover. She would be whole. And happy. I'd make sure of that. "My baby."

"Yes, he's yours. Of course, he is." She nodded and I looked to the sleeping infant. "I even named him after you." The softness in her voice broke me and I sank down next to her on the exam table, pulled her into my arms. We'd made him. Of course, he was perfect. Jori would grow up big, strong and become a powerful Warlord.

I had never felt like this before. Elation, joy, happiness. Sheer bliss. Also, a hint of male satisfaction and pride that my seed was fertile enough to get Gabriela with child the first and only time I took her. I wanted to carry her off to the nearest bed and take her again, fill her with my seed and prove how perfect we were together.

The doctor waved a wand over Gabriela's belly. "May I see?" he asked. "I'm detecting metal."

Gabriella moved her hand and lifted

the hem of her shirt a few inches and pushed down the top of her pants.

"What the fuck is that?" I growled, looking at the angry looking incision that had to be at least seven inches across. The wounded flesh was marred by metal pieces, the soft skin I'd licked and kissed as I'd worked my way down to her pussy now torn and bruised.

"My incision," Gabriela said. "It looks fine."

"Fine? *Fine?* That's not fine. What kind of barbarians do you have on Earth? You look like you've been attacked by a knife!"

"I was. It's how your fourteen-pound son got out of my body," Gabriela countered, then put her clothes back in place.

"But you're not healed and it's been a week!" I couldn't allow my mate to be like this. "This is why you look so weak. You are not well, mate."

"Jorik, you don't have to point out how horrible I look," she countered, her gaze dropping away. "I gave birth to a watermelon. I was cut open and sewed back up, then sent home to take care of him. Alone. My milk has come in and I'm telling you, that was a surprise. I'm still bleeding from the birth, so sex is totally off the table. I don't remember the last time I showered, let alone brushed my teeth or even combed my hair. Your baby eats constantly, and I've barely slept in over a week."

I glanced at the doctor. "Is this normal?"

"She is from a primitive planet," he replied, as if that explained everything.

I'd been stationed there a few months and had to agree, although I had never considered how they birthed their children.

"There are no ReGen pods on Earth. No postpartum pod protocol," the doctor said. "Those are, I believe, called staples."

"Yes. And inside I have dissolvable stitches," Gabriela clarified.

"Inside?" I couldn't let her remain like this a moment longer. "She must go in a ReGen pod now. I won't allow her to be in pain and injured a moment longer."

"I did have a pain pill before I left Earth, but... yeah, it's not like I can get the prescription filled here."

The doctor nodded. "I agree." He looked kindly at Gabriela. "When a female gives birth on a Coalition planet, she is put in a ReGen pod to heal all wounds from delivery. It is not painful. In fact, it is restful, restorative and quick."

"How does it work?" she asked.

"The pod puts you to sleep and it heals you," the doctor replied simply. "There are detailed scientific explanations for the process, but that's basically it. No more pain. No more bleeding. Your body will be completely healed of all birth trauma."

"Are you serious? It sounds like a miracle. How long does it take?"

"Depends on the level of injury. For a surgical birth like this, perhaps an hour. After that, your body will be rid of all ill effects of the birth. No pain pills you mentioned. No staples. As I said, your body will be completely healed."

"Can it zap off the extra baby weight?"

I frowned, wondering why my mate wished to remove any bit of her lush curves.

The doctor chuckled. "I'm afraid the ReGen pod will heal your body, but it does not remove healthy cells."

"You will do no such thing, mate." I wrapped my hand around the base of her skull, tilted her weary face to mine. "I love every inch of you. You will not speak of such a thing."

"I'm too big, Jorik." Tears gathered in her eyes again.

My beast growled, and I leaned down to kiss her. Gently. My touch soft. She was fragile, right now. Hurting. Tired. So beautiful I struggled to breathe. I could not bear to see her suffer. "You are perfect."

She looked to the baby, who was still sleeping in the governor's arms. He'd remained remarkably quiet through all this. "I'll still be able to nurse?"

"Of course."

She looked undecided, but I understood. If they told me I had to go into a ReGen pod right now, I wouldn't want it either. I would be petrified my mate and baby would disappear.

"I will remain right here at your side. I won't leave," I vowed. "I will hold the baby the entire time. I promise you, my beast will not allow either of you to be far from me." In fact, he snarled at me to get our mating cuffs on her as soon as possible. Then she'd be locked to us, officially mated. Mine forever. No one would question our union once I wore the mating cuffs. More, I wanted everyone to know I was hers. That she'd blessed me with a child. That we were a family.

But there would be an unavoidable delay. I had refused to bring mating cuffs to The Colony once I'd heard Gabriela had chosen a new mate. I hadn't believed I would need them. I could request a pair from the S-Gen machine, but the best craftsmen on Atlan had always made the best cuffs by hand. I wanted Gabriela to have the best. The very best.

And now that she was here, I could put in a requisition, have the cuffs delivered within a day.

I could wait if it meant the cuffs would be as beautiful as the female they would adorn. Once an Atlan male put the cuffs around his wrists, he never removed them. Ever. To do so could trigger a killing frenzy in his beast even if he had not suffered from Mating Fever when he'd chosen his female.

I looked at *my* chosen female. She had not been matched to me by a computer, but she was mine all the same. Perfect for me. I knew it, and so did my beast.

But then, how had she married another? How had she arrived here, with my son? I had many questions, but they could wait. Gabriela's pain was not to be tolerated.

She shifted in my arms and winced.

"God, that feels like someone just stabbed me with a knife. I could really use a pain pill right now."

"There is no need, I promise you." The doctor helped with more reassurance. "Jori will be fine during your recovery. I will look him over, but you did all the hard work." The doctor set a reassuring hand on top of Gabriela's. "I'll give him an exam, make sure he is doing well after the transport. Then you can both rest without worry in your private quarters."

She tipped her head back to look at me with worried eyes. "Should I, Jorik?"

"Go into the ReGen pod?"

She nodded, weak, hurting, leaving the choice to me, trusting me to take care of her. My heart swelled until the pain choked me. I did not deserve such faith, not after leaving her pregnant and alone. I did not deserve *her,* but I wasn't going to give her up.

"Yes, mate," I murmured. "Do not be afraid. When you get out, you will be completely healed. No more pain."

"It would be great to feel normal again."

My beast growled, and I knew she felt the rumble of it against her back. "Yes, and then we can work on making our daughter."

She laughed at me, even patted my cheek in a patronizing way. "Jorik, I don't think I'll ever want to have sex again, and I can't imagine you looking at this body with desire any time soon."

"You will see, mate," I told her, eager to prove her wrong. I already wanted her, my cock already hard. Every curve and hollow mine to explore. Mine. "One hour and you will see."

9

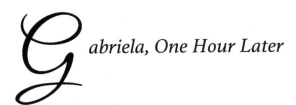
abriela, One Hour Later

IT WAS the second time that day I opened my eyes and Jorik was there. I blinked, just to be sure.

He smiled at me, that handsome face focused completely on me. I took in those chocolate colored eyes, the dark hair, even the stubble on his square jaw. He looked even more rugged than ever. Even more perfect.

"Mate," he whispered. "How do you feel?"

I turned my head, remembered I was in the fancy pod thingy. I was comfortable, lying upon a soft cushion, the base metal, the top, which was up, reminded me of a fighter jet's curved, clear window. Jorik leaned over me, his hand gripping the side.

I shifted a little and he helped me to sit up. I didn't feel any sharp pain from my C-section incision, nor did I feel tired.

"Careful," the doctor warned as he came into the room. After agreeing to the space treatment, Jorik had carried me into a different room in the medical center where multiple pods were lined up. Two of them had their lids closed, people—aliens—inside. Two more had been empty. Until me. "Your Earth staples were removed while you slept and the ReGen pod has done its work. You should be feeling much better."

He nodded approvingly as I pushed down my ratty sweatpants to inspect the damage. There was no barely healed incision. No scar. No pain. Nothing.

"Oh my god. It's gone."

The baby made a funny sound and I looked to him, tucked up tightly against Jorik's chest. He was still wrapped in the soft blanket I'd grabbed when Warden Egara had come to the apartment. For being such a huge newborn, he looked tiny in Jorik's hold. He was lying across his father's forearm, his arms and legs on either side, his head up by the crook of his elbow. He stared at me with his dark eyes. I doubted they'd ever change to a different color.

"Hi, love," I whispered, smiling at him. He was too little to smile at me, although he stilled when he recognized my voice.

"We've been sitting here getting to know each other while the pod worked on you," Jorik said, his voice so calm. I remembered when he'd gone crazy during the robbery and this... god, he was so different. So gentle. Lifting his arm, he kissed little Jori's head. "I changed his diaper, although I wasn't exactly sure about the odd Earth one."

"You have a very low opinion of everything from Earth," I said.

"Everything except you," he countered and those eyes... god, I could get lost in them.

"I did scans on him and he's perfect," the doctor said, smiling at Jori. "It isn't often we have newborns here. Only a few so far. He is a treat for the entire planet." He looked to me. "All these tough fighters are going to turn into comedians the moment they see him."

Jorik didn't disagree, just looked to me and smiled.

"As for you," he continued. "Besides the incision, did you have any other discomforts from your birth that have lingered? How's your back? Sore nipples?"

I looked to the doctor as Jorik snuggled little Jori with a unreadable expression on his face. Having a huge Prillon warrior ask about my nipples was a bit embarrassing, but he was a doctor, just like mine. And he kept his tone so professional that I answered him without thinking, even though Jorik had frozen, motionless, with the doctor's question.

"My back is better. Carrying around a watermelon definitely tweaked it. My nipples are better." I cleared my throat, sure I was turning red as a strawberry. Time to change the subject. "I feel... rested. Like I slept twelve hours."

"What's wrong with your nipples?" Jorik asked, eyeing my chest.

My nipples definitely weren't sore any longer—they'd been chapped and uncomfortable from Jori's nursing. Now, they were hard and my breasts were achy for a reason other than the baby lying content in his father's arms.

My face heated. "Your son is just like you." When he frowned, I continued, "He's obsessed with my breasts."

Jorik grinned wickedly. "I shall see to them myself. I will be a very *hands on* mate."

The doctor ignored Jorik's plan to monitor my nipples himself.

"Your son will still want to eat around the clock and sleep will be hard to find for a few more months until he's on a schedule, but you won't have to worry about a long recovery on top of that now."

Convinced of the miracle that was a ReGen pod, I let go of the elastic waistband. "Do the other mothers nurse? Do you have formula here? I might want a break once in a while. Or..." I looked at Jorik, thinking of how I might like to spend some quality alone time with my man. "A babysitter?"

The doctor smiled. "Human infant nutritional needs have been programmed into the S-Gen units. All you have to do is request it, as you do any other food item."

"Wow." So, no cooking? I was loving this place already.

"Do you wish for another child right away?" the doctor asked. "If not, there are several birth control options I can offer you."

My mouth fell open. I never considered birth control because I'd been alone on Earth. But now, with Jorik? I'd gotten pregnant the first—and only—time we'd had sex. I didn't think I could get pregnant eight days after giving birth, but Jorik was virile and I was obviously pretty fertile. I wouldn't put it past him to knock me up right away.

I looked to him, but he remained silent, letting me make the decision.

"I definitely want to hold off for a while."

"I'll give you a shot and you will be protected for six months. I'll remind you once it's time to renew the treatment, and you can make any changes then."

Once that was done, Jorik said, "Come, mate. Let's get you out of here and to my quarters. I have plans."

That involved my nipples. Worked for me. Unlike an hour earlier—or however long I'd been in the pod—I had interest in sex. I felt attraction. Desire. Need. Except for the fact I hadn't showered in...

light years and my hair was probably snarled.

Jorik scooped me up and I squealed his name. "Don't smoosh the baby!"

He set me back on my feet when I smacked his shoulder. "The baby is fine. You think me so weak I can't carry my mate and my child?"

I felt better. Recovered, as if I hadn't had major surgery eight days ago. But my boobs were still big, heavy and full of milk. The pod hadn't returned me to pre-pregnancy state, only healed me from the birth.

I leaned forward, kissed Jori's soft head, then looked up... way up, at Jorik. "I am so happy. I feel better. God, just seeing you, knowing you're alive..."

Tears filled my eyes. Again, for what felt like the thousandth time since I'd met him. But it wasn't exhaustion or hormones or the terrified feeling I'd had when I realized I was pregnant and all alone. This was... agony. Bittersweet. Overwhelming. Looking at Jorik hurt.

Touching him hurt. I'd grieved him, lived with his loss for almost a year. And now?

Now he was forcing a dead heart to beat again. To *feel*. To *love* him. To risk losing him again.

Jorik leaned down and whispered close to my ear. "You are what kept me alive in captivity, Gabriela. I thought of you. Of your smile, your voice, your body. The way you melted like your Earth ice cream at my touch. The way you sounded when you came. How you felt around my cock."

"Jorik," I whispered back, looking over my shoulder to see if the doctor had overheard, but he was gone.

"You said earlier you never wished to have sex again. Is this still true?" His voice sent shivers down my spine. I wasn't cold, I was... very hot.

"That pod thing is a miracle worker," I replied.

He grinned. "That wasn't an answer, mate."

"I want to have sex again. Soon. But

first, I need a shower. Badly. And Jori will want to eat."

"I want to eat, too. I am not keen on sharing you, mate, but I will. For him. But I will be sure to taste you a little lower."

Oh. My. God.

My alien beast was back. My libido was back. And they were together.

It was go-time for sex.

∼

Jorik

WHILE I WISHED to carry Gabriela all the way to our—fuck yes, *our*—quarters, I wrapped my arm about her shoulders and held her closely to me instead, allowing her to walk.

I was confident the ReGen pod had healed her body, but seeing the wounds, what she'd gone through at the hands of the barbaric doctors on Earth, to have our baby... I wanted to go there and rip off more heads.

She'd been in pain. She'd been cut open and left to heal with nominal pain suppressants. She'd been alone. The knowledge that she'd carried and delivered Jori all by herself made my beast lower his head in shame, but it also made him fiercer than ever.

Gabriela was here. She was mine. She wasn't going fucking anywhere, and she would never suffer again.

When we came upon my entry, there stood Governor Rone and his mate, Rachel, waiting for us. "The doctor told me you two were headed back to your quarters," he said, explaining how he knew when to show up.

Seeing us, Rachel came over to us with an excitement bordering on giddy.

"Another Earth woman. And a *baby!*"

. But her smile was infectious, and her mate shared her happiness.

As did I. My beast preened at showing off the baby Gabriela and I had made.

"I'm Rachel and I was matched to this guy." She tilted her head toward the governor who wore his Prillon mating collar with pride. They were a matched pair with copper collars around their necks. "I'm also matched to Ryston, but he's working."

"I'm Governor Rone, but you can call me Maxim. I have to admit, I am *very* pleased you are here."

Gabriela glanced between the two of them. "Nice to meet you. I'm sorry I'm such a slob."

"Woman, you have a week-old newborn. I'm surprised you can speak coherently. Besides, you should have seen Jorik before you showed up," Rachel said. "God, he was a hot mess. Tearing through everyone but Tyran in the fighting pits."

My beast growled because she was right. I'd been insane. I'd have killed someone before much longer. "Tyran has godlike strength, Lady Rone. No one on this planet can best him in hand to hand combat."

"Don't I know it. You fighting males are hot." She leaned into the governor's shoulder, her eyes glazing with desire. I knew that look on a human female. Her mate's sharp Prillon features came to distinct focus as his mate's need hit him full force.

Lucky male. As was I. Time to get rid of our well-meaning visitors.

"I am not overheated." I looked at Gabriela, who was smiling, enjoying the teasing at my expense. I was happy to suffer, to put that look on her face. "And I was not a mess. I simply needed my mate."

"Down, boy," Rachel teased. "And I think Gabriela would disagree, about your level of hotness." She did something funny with her eyebrows, lifting them up and down.

Gabriela laughed. "Are there more women from Earth here?"

Rachel smiled. "Yep. You make eight females. One's a toddler."

Gabriela's smile faded. "On the whole planet?"

"Not sure. But that's it for us here on Base 3. Estrogen is hard to find around here, but we have girls' night every other week in my quarters. I'll make sure you get the invite."

"Thank you."

"You're welcome. We took the time while you were healing to get baby things for you," Rachel added. "A crib and a few other items to get you through the next day or two, but then you can S-gen whatever else you might need."

"That's very thoughtful," Gabriela replied.

"If you'll excuse us," I began, not all that interested in talk of cribs. "We have some catching up to do."

"Oh, I know that means you're going to have lots of sex," Rachel said. "Why don't we babysit for you?"

"No." Gabriela and I said the one word at the same time, both of us equally adamant.

"I am not letting them out of my sight," I told the governor and Lady Rone.

"I'm sure you're super nice and all, but Jori's going to be hungry soon and it might be best—"

"Let them be, mate," Governor Rone said, his voice almost sweet, a tone he only used with Rachel. "The baby is newly born. I doubt Gabriela will allow him away from her. Besides, she needs to adjust to not only new people, but a new planet. As for Jorik, you saw him. You think he'll allow his child to be away from his protection?"

Rachel sighed. "I understand. Think of us if you change your mind. Keep us in mind... *first*. I think you'll have plenty of volunteers who will want to get their hands on that cute little guy for some quality snuggling."

"Thank you, Lady Rone," I said, trying to be as respectful as possible when all I wanted to do was go in our quarters, lock the door and turn off all comms for the next week. Gods, the next month. Year, even.

I wanted Gabriela all to myself and no one was getting near Jori, let alone holding him. Thank gods Gabriela didn't have a girl. The governor would have had to lock me up, for sure.

When the couple walked away, Gabriela said, "Shower, Jorik. Please."

10

 orik

I HAD JORI, who was sound asleep, settled on the bathing room floor, lying on a folded blanket as a cushion. He was within reach, but I could focus solely on Gabriela. I assisted her with her clothing, let each piece drop to the floor until she stood bare before me.

"Jorik," she whispered, using her arms to cover herself.

I took her wrists, pulled them away so

I could look my fill. I hadn't had much opportunity in her apartment to gaze upon her gorgeous body, for we'd both been too frantic to go slow.

But now I could. I could take the rest of our lives to learn every inch of her.

My mouth watered to taste every inch of her.

I told her that and her eyes shifted from wariness to heat.

"Shower first, taste second."

Remembering she'd only arrived on The Colony, never being anywhere other than Earth, I turned on the bathing tube and helped her in. We would not fit in together, so I watched as the water made her dark skin glisten, the bubbles from the soap slide down her body. I wanted her hands to be mine. And when she tipped her head back to wash her long hair...

"Hurry, mate," I growled. My beast, now confident Gabriela was here to stay, began to prowl once again, eager to make her ours.

The water slid through her black hair like a waterfall of dark temptation. I'd always loved her hair, but it seemed thicker now, shinier. Her breasts were larger and full, heavy for my son. Her rounded stomach and ass were curvier, softer, and I could not stop my beast from reaching into the spray of water to place a heavy palm on her abdomen where she'd carried my child.

I'd missed her pregnancy and birth, missed seeing her grow with our child, then the birth, when he'd taken his first breath. Her body was a machine, a miracle-maker. I'd been integrated, at least partially, by the Hive, but they would never be able to do what Gabriela had accomplished.

She'd given me a gift I could never repay, and I trembled with the need to sink into her softness, feel her warm and supple body accept mine in every way. I was hard, harder now that the Hive had fed me their contaminated technology. My muscles were no longer purely cells and blood, but microscopic technology I could never hope to remove.

"Jorik." Gabriela leaned into my touch, wrapped her hands over mine. "I'm sorry. I'm not the same—"

I cut her off, unwilling to hear her apologize for being beautiful, for carrying my son. "You are a gift, mate. And you are beautiful. Even more beautiful now than you were before. Every curve, every mark on your body is precious to me. I am not the same either. We have been through much while apart. We are different, but we know each other."

I pulled her from the shower and turned off the water, uncaring if she considered herself clean enough. I'd waited. I'd watched her touch every inch of her skin with quiet efficiency. Now, I would touch every inch with heat. Lust. Worship.

Before, on Earth, I'd needed her. My beast had wanted her for his own. Now, with my son on the floor behind me and his mother in my arms, I was complete in a way I'd never dreamed possible. She had given me more than love, more than peace. She had given me something to fight for. Something to live for.

She'd taken a male lost in dark despair and given me hope. She'd been my key to survival, my drive, my fight, my *dream* as the Hive had tortured me. Every moment had been worth it, for it brought me here to her.

Love was too weak a word for what poured from my chest to the rest of my body, and I dropped to my knees, the pain so intense that I could no longer stand as I wrapped a towel around her. All the days and months of torture, all the rage and terror I'd felt at the hands of the Hive, all burst through me now that I knelt before her. A purge. Agony sizzled through my veins, mental and physical, a tidal wave of destruction I'd been holding back by sheer force of will. That destruction had appeared in the fighting pits, in the razor's edge of control I'd held over my beast, but now I gave in to the anguish and allowed it to wash over me.

As I'd known she would, Gabriela stood, a goddess in my eyes, and wrapped her arms around me, held me together as I broke into a million pieces.

I cried, and I never cried. Not since I was still clinging to my mother's dress as a small child. But as much as I needed my mate, my beast needed her more.

The transformation struck hard and fast, and I didn't try to fight it. My beast was scarred, broken, he'd suffered the brunt of our time with the Hive Integration units and their experiments. He'd endured. He'd raged. He'd kept me alive— and sane.

And he'd suffered.

This comfort Gabriela gave was for him, not me, and I let him take it, let our mate make us both whole again as we broke down in front of the only person in the universe we could give ourselves to completely, without fear of judgment.

"Mate." My beast spoke that one word as I grew. My arms tightened where I'd wrapped them around her waist, my beast's head now cradled in the soft curve of her neck. And my beast shuddered as silent tears ran down her soft skin in a river to soak her towel.

Gabriela's hand lifted to my—our—head and she stroked the beast, pet him like he was precious and tender, not a monster to be feared. Her touch soothed, her voice, whatever she was crooning, eased. We knelt before her for what felt like hours and gave her our pain, soaked in her softness and her scent, her acceptance of every broken part of us. We allowed her to heal us in a way I'd never thought possible.

And then my son demanded his mother's attention, fussing then letting up a scream my beast was proud of. That beast, however, was not willing to give up any part of Gabriela. And he had not yet met his son.

Turning, I lifted the tiny boy into my arms, then stood, carrying both him and his mother into the other room. When I had them settled in my lap, where I could watch my son eat, my beast nuzzled Gabriela's cheek. "Feed him."

"What?" She looked up at me, startled, and I saw the tears in her own eyes for the first time. She'd been crying with me. Hurting with me. Sharing my pain.

"No more sad. Feed Jori. I watch." My beast was trying very hard to be eloquent, but he wanted to watch his son feed at his mother's breast, wanted to hold them both in his arms, protecting them. Admiring the perfect baby he'd helped create, that was part of him. I didn't disagree. I wanted to watch as well. The moment was so intimate, so unlike any moment before. I'd never experienced anything remotely close to the feeling of pride and contentment I felt with my mate and my son in my—my beast's—arms. "Feed. I watch."

Gabriela wiped her tears away and smiled shyly. "Okay. It's not that exciting."

I disagreed. "Beautiful."

She did as I'd asked, and Jori settled down at once, latching on like his life depended on it. I supposed it did. I craned my neck. I didn't want to miss a single thing. Not the sweet sounds Jori made, or the look on my mate's face when she stared down at our son.

Pure, unconditional love.

When she lifted her gaze to my beast's, that look didn't change, and my beast's protective instincts turned to desire in the space of a heartbeat, my cock growing hard as a rock where her soft ass rested in my lap. "Mate."

"Jorik." She leaned back, the babe at her breast as I looked my fill. Little Jori stared wide-eyed and dazed when she lifted him to her shoulder and patted his back, then placed him on the other side to finish feeding. I was in no hurry to end this bliss, but I anticipated the moment little Jori would go in his crib and his mother would be mine.

All mine.

A few minutes later, my cock was pounding, the beast had no intention of allowing me to regain control. This was his time, his turn. He wanted to fuck our female, fill her with his cock, make her beg and writhe and scream. I did not fear her health now. The ReGen pod had done its job. She was no longer pale, dark circles were no longer smudged beneath her eyes. The ruthless incision was gone. All pain, all discomfort had disappeared. All that was left was a healthy, aroused mate.

My beast wanted her to place the mating cuffs around my wrists and claim us for her own, but the cuffs would not arrive until tomorrow. I'd ordered them from Atlan as she slept in the pod. I did not want to delay, but my beast was content to wait, assured that she was ours now. Our mate. Our female. Our son.

She stood and went over to the small crib in the next room, I could see her through the open doorway as she bent over it to settle Jori for sleep. The towel I'd wrapped around her hung on her hips. Barely. She walked back into our sleeping quarters, leaving the door open so we could hear Jori if he began to cry.

Her top was bare, her breasts full, the nipples inflamed and peaked from the feeding. I wanted that. All of it. My beast agreed.

"Mine." I stripped off my clothes, ready and eager.

She paused in the doorway, looked her fill.

"You... you don't have any integrations," she said.

My cock rose from just her gaze on me. "Inside." One word. I'd tell her more later. Right now, my beast had other things on his mind.

She seemed content with the answer, and I would not delay any longer.

The beast moved so quickly she gasped as I lifted her in the air and walked forward, pressing her back to the wall of my quarters. Her towel fell to the floor leaving her completely bare. I didn't have mating cuffs, but I had the usual Atlan model restraints every beast preferred. A beast did not fuck lying down, the position making him too vulnerable to attack.

It was a survival instinct. And so our females adapted. When the beast was in command, he was not tender.

He devoured. Conquered. Claimed.

"Oh my god, what?" Gabriela's nervous laughter slowed down my beast, but not much, as he clamped her wrists and bent thighs to the wall, spreading her open for us, her perfect pussy on display for a feast. The restraints around her thighs were well padded and large enough to hold an Atlan female. They would support her slight human body without a problem, freeing my beast to roam. Explore. Taste.

"Stop?" My beast would stop, if she asked it of him, but I prayed she would not. He was holding on by a thread, the pain he'd shared with her earlier replaced by a desperate hunger for pleasure.

"Don't stop," she breathed. "Don't ever stop."

I dropped to my knees and sucked her clit into my mouth, feasting on what was mine. She bucked, her hips fighting to get closer.

"Oh, god. More."

With a growl, I complied, opening her body with one hand, fucking her with my fingers of the other as I worked her with my mouth, devoured the wet heat that was mine, and mine alone. The taste of her made my beast howl in happiness, and I knew we would never forget her flavor, her scent.

"Mine."

"Yes." She seemed to sense that my beast needed to hear her say the word, hear her surrender.

Remembering how she'd clamped down with pleasure, how she'd screamed the one time I took her on Earth, I slipped the tip of one finger inside her ass and played.

"Jorik!" she cried at the intimate act, but nothing was shameful between us. If she desired it, I would give it to her. This female was mine to pleasure, and my beast was going to make even the gods bow to his mastery of her body.

Gabriela

OH MY FUCKING GOD. He was going to kill me.

I was spread open and on display and he knelt at my pussy, his mouth feasting like I was his favorite treat. I'd never been restrained before, never held open like this, never completely at a man's—alien's —mercy.

And the greedy bitch inside me wanted more. I couldn't move—and that turned me on. I trusted Jorik with my life, knew he would stop if I asked. I felt safe. Cherished. And that made me lose my fucking mind.

I'd been shy before Jori's birth, but once I'd survived that, some of my self-conscious nature had died off. But with

Jorik, my mate? His eyes didn't lie. He wanted me. He didn't just like what he saw, he *wanted* to touch me. Kiss me. Make me come. His touch was deliberate and dominant, as if he knew exactly what he wanted.

Me.

So fucking hot. I'd never been this out of control, and that knowledge sent my body racing.

I was stunned by the ReGen pod, how it had healed my incision completely, had taken away all discomfort from the birth. I felt rejuvenated. Oh, I still had the extra weight, but Jorik seemed to like it. I had to let go of all hang ups because, to him, I had none. I had to give over to Jorik, which was fine by me.

I didn't want to be in control. I wanted to belong to Jorik.

When he spread me open with his fingers and suckled my clit, flicking his tongue over me, I gave him everything, my body exploding as his growl of satisfaction pushed me harder, sending pulse after pulse of orgasm through my entire being.

My body jerked against the restraints. I wanted to touch him. Ride him. Kiss him.

"Jorik!" I was begging, but I wasn't sure what I wanted. What I needed. Him. Just him. This was what I'd craved in those months of separation. The scent of him, the feel, the wild abandon in his every touch. I'd missed him so much.

"More." The deep voice of his beast made my pussy clench as he slid a second finger inside my still spasming pussy, fucking me a bit harder, spreading me open as he kissed his way up my body as I tried to catch my breath. He placed a tender kiss on each nipple, before licking and nibbling his way up to my neck. My lips.

He stopped. Held. I opened my eyes and stared into the gaze of the beast, the male I loved buried deep, but still there. *This* was Jorik. All of him. And he waited. For what? Permission? Acceptance?

His fingers slid in and out of my pussy as we stared into each other's eyes, the beast waiting for something.

"Kiss me. Fuck me. Do it. I want you. I want all of you." I made sure I was clear, unblinking as I made my own demands. "You're mine, Jorik. Mine."

His beast's smile was predatory and my pussy clamped down on his fingers. Hard.

"Oh, god." I was going to come again.

"No god. Jorik." He pressed his thumb to my clit and circled. I screamed his name as I came.

Pussy still spasming, his huge cock pressed inside, opened me slowly.

He was huge. Really damn big, and I gasped, half in shock, half in pain as he filled me. Stretched me. Claimed me.

He was too big. Too much. My pussy too tight, too swollen, too sensiti—

"Ahhhh!" I came again, the orgasm ripping through me like a zap of electric current. No warning. No build-up. Just him. I rippled around him, dripped all over his cock and eased his way.

"Jorik." His beast groaned as my pussy clamped down and he pumped into me, in and out, slowly, then gaining in speed as he filled me completely. "Mine."

"God, yes."

He stopped moving. Frowned. The most adorable expression on a beast. "No god. Jorik. Mate."

"Yes, love. Jorik." I loved him. Holy shit, did I love him. I loved his son. I loved his cock. I loved how beautiful I felt when I was with him. I loved being at his mercy, knowing I was beautiful, desirable. Perfect. "Mate."

That appeased him and he fucked me in earnest, my back sliding up the wall with each thrust of his massive body. I was at his mercy, shackled to the wall, and I never wanted it to stop. I was trapped, and if I had an inner beast, she would howl. I wasn't going anywhere. I couldn't. No one was taking me from Jorik.

His scent surrounded me. His heat.

His power. He was strong, so strong. And he was mine.

I gave in at that moment, the tears streaking down my face. I surrendered the very last piece of my wounded heart, the heart that had lived in fear, the heart that had broken when I'd thought he'd died, the heart that would kill to protect our son. I gave it to him, every miserable, wilted piece of it, and my body with it.

I came again, sobbing, completely out of control. I didn't have anything left. I was broken and remade and it hurt. It fucking hurt, but I couldn't stop it. Couldn't stop myself. I was whole, here on some strange planet with him. As long as we were together, him, me, the child we made, I didn't care where we were.

He shouted out, the deep roar filling our small chamber with sound as he filled me with his seed. Marked me. Claimed me.

Again.

But this time, there was no robbery, no Hive, no war. No laws. Just us. Us and Jori.

When we could breathe again, my beast removed the restraints and carried me to bed. He wrapped his arms around me and didn't ask about my tears, for which I was thankful. I wouldn't have been able to explain them to him anyway.

Loving someone this much hurt like hell. But there was no taking it back.

And I didn't want to.

11

*G*abriela, *The Next Morning*

ATLANS WERE FORMIDABLE. Huge. Dominant. They had an intense gaze that could scare the pants off someone. They definitely scared the pants off me, and in a *very* good way. Well, not all of them. Just one Atlan in particular. And when he got my pants off... he was even more dominant, and huge in *all* the right places. I should have been exhausted since my two guys kept me up all night.

Jori had suffered no effects from the transport, consistently hungry and eager for snuggles no matter if it were day or night. The same went for his father. Jorik was consistently hungry... for me, and I hadn't been out of his arms all night. This morning, I'd woken up on top of him, my head resting in the crook of his shoulder. I didn't remember climbing on top of him, or if Jorik had settled me there, but next to him hadn't been close enough.

I had never spent the night with Jorik. We'd really only been together a few hours. I should have been uncomfortable in a bed with someone so large... heck, with someone at all, but I hadn't. I'd slept hard, even after the rejuvenating time in the pod thing. Perhaps for the first time in months, in almost a year, I wasn't sad. I wasn't alone.

My body had twinges of discomfort. Muscles ached I didn't even know I had. It wasn't as if I'd ever been bound to a wall before and well-fucked. The well-fucked part had my pussy aching and I had to admit, a little tender. But I didn't care. It made me smile. It meant Jorik had had me. That we were together.

God, I was a *total* sap.

After showering in the fancy tube-thing—God, it had a mode that dried my hair ridiculously fast—and feeding Jori, he'd miraculously made me a dress from some machine on the wall. It was flowy and soft, a pretty blue color. A typical Atlan dress, he'd said, and by his look once I had it on, he was pleased to see me in it.

So pleased he'd tried to take it off. I'd resisted, barely, because we'd never leave his quarters if I didn't, so instead, he dropped to his knees before me, lifted the long hem and put his mouth on me. To say he was wicked with his tongue... god, I was hot now thinking about it. As for resisting and telling him no? What woman in her right mind would say no to a gorgeous Atlan wanting to eat her pussy?

Not me.

After I'd recovered—and he'd wiped his mouth of the glistening proof of how much I liked his attention—he took us to the main food area, a cafeteria of sorts, for breakfast. When we came through the silent-sliding doors of the cafeteria, the scent of mysterious food made my stomach grumble. The space was large, with perhaps thirty tables, although I didn't see any kitchen. One whole wall was made of glass... or what looked like glass, and it was the first true glimpse I had of the planet. I really *was* in space.

There was no blue sky, no clouds. It looked kind of like I imagined Mars would, red, barren rocks, strange colored plants that looked they were hanging on to life by a thread, and above it all? Stars. Black space. It felt barren. Exposed. And I was suddenly very thankful for the dome that covered our heads, that kept us safe and protected. The landscape was beautiful, in a strange way, but it wasn't the wetlands, or the beach.

A little squeak from Jori had me turning back to him and Jorik. I smiled as Jori somehow got his hand in his mouth and was sucking on it. The only time I'd held him since we'd arrived on the planet was to feed him. Otherwise, he slept in a space version of a bassinet in a small room near Jorik's side of the bed—because he'd said he wanted our son to be within his arm's reach—or actually in his arms. Like now. He wouldn't let me hold him, and I wouldn't deny him the pleasure. It made me happy to see him do so. A huge beast brought down by a fourteen-pound newborn.

Immediately, we were bombarded. Warriors who had cyborg parts for eyes or arms like in a scary sci-fi movie came up to us, their gazes going tender and soft for Jori. I had to wonder what they'd been through, and I wondered again about

Jorik's answer when I'd asked. *Inside.* I had no idea what they'd put him through, and I doubted he'd ever tell me everything. Then again, he didn't need to relive that horror. Not for me.

I wouldn't ask that of him. But he and the other Atlans he'd been with were different. They didn't have any of the obvious mechanical or robotic features the others had. Somehow, that seemed worse.

Warden Egara had given me a quick rundown of The Colony, that those who'd been taken by the Hive, integrated in some way, lived here. Originally, everyone had been banished and forced to remain on The Colony forever, but from what she'd said, times had changed, and they could return to their home planet, although most remained.

Jorik was here and I wondered if he wanted to return to Atlan. Would we stay here on The Colony or go elsewhere? I didn't care as long as we were together.

One big guy, I assumed Atlan, waved a

cyborg hand and made googly sounds at Jori. It was so incongruous, but sweet. Jorik made a harrumphing sound and stepped back.

They'd been through so much and yet they reveled in the simple things. A baby was completely innocent, unaware of the Hive, of death, destruction. Jori was completely perfect and unbiased. If we remained here, he would grow up familiar with Hive integrations, think nothing of them. To him, all of these men would be *normal.*

"I've never seen Jorik like this," Rachel said, coming up to me and whispering in my ear. "You're like magic for him."

"I think it might be the baby," I replied. He wasn't carrying *me* around. I was off to the side, out of the way. That thought was silly because he knew exactly where I was, and I had no doubt if I even sneezed, Jorik would be at my side, looming, perhaps even dragging me back to that ReGen pod.

If I thought Jorik was protective of me, I'd been wrong. He took it to the extreme with Jori. We stared at my mate, watching as he stood in the center of the room, proud as could be, showing off his infant son. When someone got too close, he held out his arm to keep him away. When someone asked to hold Jori, he said *no* in a tone so deep and threatening, I had to laugh.

Jori looked so tiny tucked into the crook of his elbow, his little arms and leg wiggling in the small outfit Rachel and Maxim had left with the other baby supplies. It was the same pale blue as my dress and was just like footy pajamas from Earth except there was no zipper. Jori looked out at everyone, but I doubted he could see much of them yet.

"He's pleased with himself," I added.

"Mmm, yeah. These guys are ridiculously dominant. I've got Prillons for mates. Two of them," she said, her fingers playing with her copper colored collar around her neck. "But Jorik is being truly ridiculous." She pouted. "I don't think I'm ever going to hold that baby of yours."

"If I wasn't his source of food, I probably wouldn't either." I laughed, thrilled Jorik was taking to fatherhood so well. "You have a baby of your own."

She sighed. "Yes, but he's not much of a *baby* any longer. I remember what it was like, having two mates trying to get me pregnant." She sighed. "Then when I was pregnant, I couldn't pick up anything. If I made any kind of funny sound, like god forbid, a fart, they'd be all over me with worry. You should have seen them at the birth." She paused, looked at me wide-eyed. "Oh, Gabriela, I'm so sorry! I'm so selfish, complaining about how attentive and loving my men are when you missed all that with Jorik. I can't believe you did all that alone."

I thought of how hard it had been, lonely. Sad. But seeing Jori for the first time... it had been incredible. My heart had opened up, and he filled it right up.

"It's all right. I had lots of drugs."

She laughed, obviously relieved my feelings hadn't been hurt. They weren't. I couldn't compare my relationship with hers. I had no doubt having two mates wasn't easy.

We watched as Jorik shifted Jori to his other arm, then glanced up at me. Smiled. "I'm surprised he let you out of your quarters. After all those months apart, I'd think he wouldn't let you get dressed." She looked me over. "Nice dress, by the way."

Another "no" came from Jorik and a disappointed Prillon went back to his seat.

"Thanks," I replied, smoothing my hands down the soft fabric. "A ReGen pod is like the best spa day ever. Add a bunch of Atlan induced orgasms and I'm a happy woman."

Rachel snorted and I grinned.

"Come on, since we're not getting anywhere near that sweet baby, I'll introduce you around."

"Don't take me too far. Jorik will probably freak if I'm out of his sight."

Rachel grinned and took my arm.

We circled the room, starting first with her second mate, Ryston, another massive male with sharp, hawk-like features and pale golden hair with eyes to match. A section of the left side of his temple and the edge of his left eye, however, was silver. Metallic. Where Jorik had no visible signs of his time with the Hive, most of the warriors here had not survived unscathed. Rachel's mates both had visible reminders of their torture. Maxim had an arm that was almost completely silver, although I could only see the hand and wrist peeking out from his long-sleeved shirt. Strange silver-blue webbing crept out from Ryston's temple forming an odd grid on the skin covering the entire left side of his face. A human man, named Denzel, had completely silver eyes, but his human mate, Melody, was tucked snuggly against his side, clearly in love with her man. Every warrior here was different, but they all had the same haunted look in their eyes, a look that faded when they saw my huge mate and his tiny son.

We approached the Atlans last, Rachel introduced an Atlan named Kai who sat with two others. Kai was golden and beautiful, like a surf god, while the others, Wulf and Egon, both had darker hair. They all looked completely human, except for the fact that they were almost seven feet tall, and would be even bigger when they turned into their beasts. A few other Atlans were scattered around, one, whom Rachel said was named Braun, sat with Rezzer and Caroline, who went by CJ, and their twins. Braun, she said, was holding off his Mating Fever, the need to take a mate or lose control of his beast.

Apparently, being with the twins helped keep his beast happy and calm. The boy was named RJ for Rezzer Junior. To make things confusing, the girl was also called CJ, for Caroline Junior. While they both were called the same thing, it wasn't too difficult to distinguish them since one was still in diapers and could barely talk. Both children toddled around on unsteady legs. Rachel told me they were not quite a year old, and I was thrilled to know that Jori would have playmates growing up.

My smile was somewhat forced as I realized what Warden Egara had told me about the Atlans was true. Compared to the number of Prillons and other races, the Atlans stood out like sore thumbs. Big. Brutish.

Alone.

Like Warlord Tane, another Atlan Rachel had pointed out. He stood off to the side, armed to the teeth as several others came up to speak to him. They, also, wore guns of some kind, and armor. Matching uniforms so I had to wonder if they were on duty, and if so, for what.

Warlord Wulf saw my interest. "They have recently returned from a hunt."

"A hunt where?" And what were they hunting, exactly? The dome kept us locked inside, where we could breathe the air. I'd been warned not to go outside without proper protection. There was an atmosphere here, but it was toxic.

"In the mines." Wulf's vocabulary matched that of my mate's. Pathetic. Three words was not going to satisfy my curiosity. It wasn't as if the Atlans weren't intelligent. They were just spare with their answers.

"And what, exactly, are they hunting in the mines? Snakes? Scorpions? Hell-hounds?" I was sure they hunted none of those things, but I did want an answer. And if I had to pull it from him, I would.

"Hive."

Oh. Shit. My mouth fell open as I looked out the big window, then glanced at Jori. Jorik had moved to stand beside us and I was glad. "They're here?"

"Not anymore."

Well, that made me feel better. Almost. I'd never imagined that the Hive might be here. On this planet. I felt my face pale, a shiver race over my skin.

Wulf stood and the other Atlans took

their cue from him, standing to form a circle around me. And Jorik. And Jori.

Braun rose from his seat—disentangling himself from the rambunctious twin climbing up his back—to join us, Rezzer with him. Tane left his post by the door and came in close.

I was surrounded by aliens—Atlans—all of them more than a foot taller than I was.

"You are safe here, Gabriela, mate of Jorik. Every one of us would die to protect you or your son. As would every warrior on this planet."

Wow. Okay. What was I supposed to say to that? They all stared, every single one of them, looking right at me. Intense was too tame a word. "Umm, thank you."

With a few grunts and nods of approval, Rezzer and Braun left us to track down the twins who'd run off somewhere, although they didn't seem concerned. This was a safe place and unless the kids ran with knives or found an alien light socket, they probably wouldn't be harmed. It was reassuring to know there was that kind of freedom here.

Tane rejoined his hunting party, and Jorik held out a seat for me at the table between himself and Kai. Wulf sat across from me, and the way the others responded to him, I knew he was their leader. Even Rezzer and Braun had treated him with respect.

The four males I sat with were the only unmarked males here. No silver. No prosthetic limbs or silver eyes. They looked completely normal, for aliens.

CJ breezed by and set a plate of piping hot lasagna in front of me. Melted mozzarella. Fresh tomato sauce. My mouth watered instantly. "Lasagna for breakfast?"

She grinned. "If you want, I can get you some alien worms or something."

That made me laugh. And I loved lasagna. Besides, somewhere on Earth it had to be dinner time. "It's five o'clock somewhere. Thank you!"

Her grin was contagious and I took the

first bite around my own smile as she continued, "Since Prime Nial is mated to one of us, you can get almost any Earth food out of the S-Gen machine. It's awesome."

I laughed, excited to know I wouldn't have to eat purple vegetables, or weird animal meat. "Even ice cream?" Man, I missed Sweet Treats, the double fudge and cookie dough, the salted caramel and pecan, the—

"Yes, and chocolate."

"Thank god." I really was relieved. And starving. Jorik had worn me out, and between his attention and nursing Jori, I was ready to mutate from pleasant to *hangry* in about five more minutes.

"Do not thank your god, female. What have I told you about that?" Jorik raised his brows as he rubbed Jori's back. How that man could be playing daddy of the year *and* reminding me of sex at the same time was a mystery.

"Remember all those times you served me ice cream?" he murmured in my ear.

I nodded.

"Every time I imagined you serving it not in a cone, but melted over your body. I wanted to lick the flavor you called strawberry off your nipples, wondered if they'd be the same bright pink."

I knew my cheeks right now were that color at his bold words.

"And lower, I wondered if you tasted as sweet. Now I know."

I swallowed hard, squirmed at how hot he made me. I didn't look his way, didn't dare or I'd probably jump him right here in the cafeteria. Instead, I devoured the lasagna, the best I'd ever tasted. And ginger tea, because even though I wasn't pregnant anymore, my stomach still had its moments. As I ate, Jorik did as well, occasionally grinning at me in the way that promised a lot of *licking* later. He was careful to make sure Jori was safe, protected, and warm. My son slept like the dead in his father's hold, and my heart swelled once more. Tears threatened and I had to look away or embarrass myself in front of all of Jorik's friends.

Instead of looking at my guys, I took the time to look around. Now that the baby wasn't the center of attention, there still were a lot of warriors gathered. Vikens. An Everian Hunter, who looked totally human, until he moved. Then it was like watching a vampire movie where the bad guys practically float across the floor and moved too fast to be remotely normal. I would have been freaked out by that, if it weren't for an adorable little boy of about six years old, who came right up to me, looked at Jori, kissed the baby on the head, and walked off without a word.

Jorik looked pleased and nodded at the Everian, who nodded back. "That is the Hunter, Kiel of Everis. And that is his son, Wyatt."

"Seems like a sweet boy," I said, surprised Jorik had let the boy kiss Jori, let alone get near him.

"He is," Jorik agreed. "He has a very dangerous father."

Coming from him, that was saying something. I looked at the man—alien—

again, wondering how someone so normal looking, so... human, could inspire that kind of respect from a beast. He had a woman sitting next to him. Lindsey, if I remembered correctly what Rachel had told me, but I hadn't met her yet. She smiled at me from across the room and I smiled back. Her response was real, the happiness going all the way to her eyes, and I knew we'd be friends.

There had to be hundreds of warriors wandering in and out of the dining area, as Jorik and the doctor had warned me. It seemed we were big news and *everyone* wanted to check out Jorik's new mate and baby. I wasn't sure I'd ever remember all their names, and definitely not right away.

"I'm glad you're here," Kai said, forking up something green and leafy. As I looked, he grinned, his face transforming from intense to charming in an instant.

Why didn't he have a mate? He was, frankly, gorgeous. Not that I was looking, but I had a couple of friends back home who would love to get their hands on someone like him.

Or Wulf.

Or Egon.

Hell, any of these guys. They were all hot hunks of alpha male, regardless of their cyborg parts. To me, it made them look hotter, more rugged, daring. Brave. And I had mine. There were plenty of lonely, disappointed women on Earth who would be more than happy to get their alien freak on. No wonder women volunteered.

Kai finished his meal and wiped his mouth with a napkin. "Before your arrival, Jorik was a little out of control. He wanted to rip my head off."

I glanced at Jorik, who shifted a now grumbling Jori to his shoulder.

"Ripping heads off? Yeah, he has a habit of doing that," I said. I doubted anyone here knew what had happened on Earth. Or maybe they did, although these Atlans didn't seem like big sharers. In fact,

I was impressed with the small bit of information Kai was offering up.

"Nothing like a female... and a baby to tame him," Kai replied. He tilted his head to the side, like a confused puppy—which was kind of adorable on a huge warrior—and looked from Jorik's wrists to me.

Jorik shook his head, but Kai didn't see the motion, he was too busy looking at me. "No mating cuffs?" He slapped Jorik on the shoulder. "Did she refuse your claim, old man?"

Mating cuffs? Refuse his claim? What was Kai talking about? Confused, I looked at Jorik, but he didn't meet my gaze.

"None of your concern. And I am far from old, Warlord. Took four of you to hold me down, as I recall."

Kai laughed as Jorik stood. Jori was fussing but he settled back down with his father's motion. It seemed it was a skill Jorik had mastered last night between feedings, letting me sleep. "Other warriors have come in and are stealing glances at our son, Gabriela. I shall introduce the newest warrior to them."

Jorik walked across the room and was instantly surrounded by those who'd come in since our arrival. I took the opportunity to look to Wulf for some kind of answer about what Kai had said. He shook his head and returned his attention to his food, clearly not going to share.

Dang Atlans!

Apparently, whatever they were talking about, I wasn't supposed to know. But why? And if there were these mating cuffs, were they like wedding rings on Earth? Did Jorik not want to claim me? Or have me claim him? Was he still unsure? Not about the baby, but about me?

Had I turned our one-night stand into something more? Last night, I thought he really loved me, but he hadn't said the words. Oh, we'd definitely had sexy times, but did that mean love? He had not spoken about claiming me, or cuffing me, or whatever it was these Atlan warriors were talking about.

Did he want me? Or did he just want Jori, and I was a side benefit? A fuck-buddy on a planet without women?

Did everyone know this, but me?

I glanced at the Atlans around me, but they were all suddenly extremely interested in their food.

The only other mated Atlan I'd met here was Rezzer. I turned to where he'd been sitting with CJ and their twins, nearly cried out when I saw the elaborate cuffs that circled both of their wrists. They were ornate. Beautiful. Impossible to miss.

Hands in my lap, I rubbed my bare wrists beneath the table. Those were *mating cuffs*. They meant something real. Permanent. And I didn't have them. Jorik had never even mentioned them to me.

Dread filled my stomach until I thought the lasagna was going to come back up.

Whatever the truth was, Jorik was definitely in love with his son. From across the room, I could see him shaking his head, a stern expression on his face. He patted Jori's back with his huge hand, shifting his body so the person before him couldn't get near him. I bit my lip, trying to stifle my reaction, not sure if it would be to laugh or cry. I knew almost nothing about this planet, about the people here, what they went through. But none of it mattered. I didn't care about anything except my guys. I knew Jorik would take care of me, see to our every need. Protect us. But was that all?

Was that enough?

With Jorik gone, I tried again to get some answers from Wulf. "Jorik said all of his integrations were on the inside." I let that statement hang in the air as I stared at Wulf willing him to tell me something useful.

"We four were the great Atlan experiment. Instead of giving us metal or external integrations, they forced our bodies to consume microscopic integrations that bonded on the cellular level. Every muscle and bone, every cell is enhanced."

What? "What does that mean? You're stronger now?"

"The doctor does not know for sure, as he has never seen this before. But we are stronger, yes. Faster to heal, our lungs can breathe the atmosphere here with no ill effects."

Wow. "That's incredible."

Warlords Egon and Kai both stopped moving, food halfway to their mouths, at my reaction.

"We are contaminated on a level never seen before. We are the worst of those here."

I shook my head and placed my hand over Wulf's. "No, you are the best of them. The strongest. Whatever the Hive did to you, you survived. And now you are miracles. Walking miracles."

Wulf looked shocked, but did not remove his hand from beneath mine. Egon and Kai resumed eating, their cheeks looking... flushed. Had I embarrassed them?

"I'm sorry. I didn't mean to offend

you." I wasn't sure what to say to make it right.

Wulf gently squeezed my hand. "You have not given offense, my lady, you have given us hope."

That made *me* blush, and I placed my hand back in my lap just as Maxim yelled.

"What?" Maxim leaped to his feet, his seat across from Rachel clattering to the floor behind him. He was speaking into what appeared to be empty space. "You've got to be fucking joking."

He stood, spun on his heel, faced Jorik. Everyone in the room went silent, watching.

"What's going on?" I whispered to Wulf.

He shrugged.

"We'll be right there," Maxim snapped, pressing a button on the side of his neck, as if he had some kind of transmission device embedded in his head.

Wait. He probably did. Just like me. The NPU Warden Egara gave me before she'd transported me and Jori here, the device that let me understand the Atlans, even though I knew they were not speaking my language.

Maxim strode over to Jorik and Rachel followed, first handing off her little boy to someone else who made funny faces at him. A cute toddler, another friend for Jori. My happiness at seeing the child quickly faded when her eyes darted to me, not with greeting or reassurance. With worry.

I stood, forgetting the Atlans at the table, and walked to Jorik and the governor. Rachel had gone completely white with shock. What was happening?

"Here. Now," Maxim said to Jorik, but I hadn't heard what he'd said before. I'd been too far away.

Jorik's eyes were wide, his skin pale. Something wasn't good. "It can't be right. Gabriela is already here," Jorik said, pulling me into his side. That motion was reassuring, but I didn't feel better.

"What's going on?" I asked.

Maxim didn't look my way, kept his

gaze on Jorik. Clenched his jaw. "I've just received word from Earth. Jorik's mate is being transported here. Now."

I glanced up at Jorik, his eyes squarely on Maxim, but his hold on me tightened.

"I don't understand, Maxim. Gabriela is already here," Rachel said.

Maxim shook his head. "No. His *Interstellar Bride.* He was tested the other day when he almost ripped the Prillon warriors to pieces in the fighting pit, before we knew of Gabriela and the baby. He wasn't removed from the IBP system when they arrived, and he has since been matched."

My heart beat frantically and I suddenly felt nauseated. He was matched... to someone else?

"That's... that's impossible," Rachel continued, pointing at us. "Look at them together. They're perfect. They even have a *baby.*"

"The testing was ninety-nine percent accurate. This female... the female who just arrived in the transport room, is his matched mate."

Then what was I? He'd been matched, with almost perfect accuracy, to another woman? Of course, he had. I thought of Jorik. So handsome. So incredible. Heroic. Gentle. Tender. Fierce. Devoted. Intelligent. Strong enough to survive months as a captive of the Hive.

Then there was me. A woman from Earth who went through hell just to finish high school. A woman with only a paycheck-to-paycheck job who'd been stupid enough to have sex without protection and get knocked up. I was here, on The Colony, not because I was the right woman for Jorik. No, I was here because of the baby.

Jori was the only reason I'd been allowed to come here, to be with Jorik. The baby was the only reason Warden Egara even knew about me. If she hadn't read the article about how big Jori was at birth... if I hadn't actually gotten pregnant, then she wouldn't have contacted me. I'd have been going about my day, walking to work scooping ice cream for tourists. Jorik would be here on The Colony. Matched. To the perfect female for him.

I had no doubt she would be amazing. Jorik was too wonderful to have anything less. I had no doubt the woman would be beautiful. Smart. Funny. Sexy.

And not me.

12

J orik

"THERE HAS TO BE A MISTAKE," I said, walking down the corridor with Gabriela, Rachel and the governor. Jori was on my shoulder, as if I'd let him out of my hold. People passed, but I paid them no attention. They looked at us, perhaps looked again, perhaps not hearing about Jori. We didn't stop, hell no. A matched mate was here? Now? For me?

The arrival of an Interstellar Bride was

always exciting news. I would welcome her to The Colony, for another male to claim. Not for me. She'd been matched to Atlan, then to me. There were many good warriors here, Atlan warriors who would be happy to care for her, pleasure her. Find their own happiness.

There was no way I was matched to another. It was impossible. Gabriela had my heart. I had no room for another female. I didn't *want* another. Neither did my beast. My entire being belonged to the small human female who walked at my side. Every cell in my body was hers. My beast agreed. He did not prowl or howl or do anything at Maxim's surprise news. He was quiet. Content because Gabriela was here, next to us, our son in our arms, my soul, for the first time in my life, at peace.

I'd washed the scent of her off in the bathing tube, but my beast didn't need to be covered in her scent to be content. He did not need the mating cuffs, although I wanted to wear them—proudly—to shout my mated status to the entire planet.

Gabriela was mine—ours—and Jori definitely proved it.

I didn't need fucking computerized intelligence to tell me who to love. I'd chosen. My beast had chosen. And Gabriela had accepted my claim. She was mine. I did not desire another. In fact, the idea of touching another female, of losing Gabriela, made my beast stir, not with desire, but with a killing frenzy. No one would take Gabriela from me and live.

The Interstellar Bride from Earth would have to choose another.

"No mistake. She just transported." Maxim picked up his pace, forcing Rachel and Gabriela to practically run to keep up with his long gait. They didn't seem to mind, all of us equally anxious to meet this female.

"From where? Atlan?" I asked. I loved the look of Gabriela in the traditional Atlan dress, and in the blue, it made my cock stir. She knew nothing of my home planet. Nothing, but I didn't care.

"No. Earth."

I heard Gabriela's quick intake of breath. I was just as surprised. If I were attracted to Gabriela, then it made sense the testing would match me to someone from the same planet. But why had I not been attracted to *all* females on Earth when I'd been there? Why Gabriela specifically? I'd thought it was because she was my mate.

No. No! She *was* my mate. There had been a mistake with the testing. This human had been transported to me by mistake. She had to belong to another.

The transport room door slid open before us and Maxim strode in first, followed by Rachel. I held out my hand to Gabriela, but she walked past me into the room. I had no choice but to follow with Jori on my shoulder. Immediately I set my gaze upon the small female who stood on the transport pad. She was my match. *Supposedly* my match.

She was small, had shoulder length light brown hair. She wore a traditional Atlan gown, as would be expected by an

Atlan warrior's bride. The gown was a light blue, nearly identical to the one I'd chosen for Gabriela just this morning.

My favorite color on a female.

The human woman turned at the sound of our arrival and I saw her face. Frowned.

"You look familiar," I said immediately. She did. But she also did not appear to be worried, nervous or surprised. She looked... almost bored, waiting for me.

She smiled, now obviously nervous and came down the steps from the raised platform. "I'm so glad. Your beast must know me already."

Her voice was soft, almost dainty.

I frowned. My beast ignored her completely, not the least bit interested. He was too busy keeping track of our mate where she hovered near the door. I was half-sure that if I weren't holding Jori, she would have run from the room already. This had to be upsetting for her. But there was no cause. She was mine and I was hers. This human female meant nothing more than a few hours inconvenience. Once the other Atlans knew she's been sent, and matched to Atlan, they'd be climbing over one another to win her over. Good, then I could go about getting deep inside Gabriela again, begging for more. Harder. Deeper.

Fuck.

Taking a tentative step toward me, the human looked about, then stopped. "I've never been to space, but I'm... I'm excited to be here, to be yours. I know I have thirty days to decide, but you are gorgeous. I won't need it. I accept your claim, Warrior."

She was that sure, after a few seconds? Nothing about this seemed... right. If she had been matched to me, my perfect match, I should have felt *something*. Surely. Anything but complete disinterest. My beast felt the same toward her as it did toward the transport tech. I looked to Maxim who, for once, looked confused.

I remembered the first time I saw Gabriela. She'd walked by the guard station on her way to work. Her hair had been pulled back, long and sleek. She'd looked at me and smiled. Those dark eyes met mine and bam. It was like an ion pistol stun. I'd frozen in place and stared. Watched her continue down the street, took in the sway of her hips, the full curve of her ass. My beast had howled. Prowled. Even panted. So had I.

But her? This Earth female who was my near perfect match?

I felt nothing. Less than nothing.

"I'm Rachel." Lady Rone stepped forward. Thankfully, she had enough brain function to be courteous. It wasn't this human's fault there'd been a mistake. Right? Rachel shook the woman's hand, then pointed at Maxim. "That guy's my mate."

"Oh, a Prillon. Only one?"

"Yes, well, he's one of my mates."

"I'm governor here," Maxim finally said, nodding to the human. "If you'll excuse me, I need to check something." He went over to the transport tech and stood beside him at his control panel.

"What's   your   name?"   Rachel asked her.

"Oh, I'm Wendy."

"You're American?"

America. One of the bride testing centers was there. In—

"I'm from Miami."

Rachel smiled, played the diplomat, greeting the poor woman who had come expecting a mate, and would be disappointed, when a flicker of memory surfaced. "You worked at the Brides Center," I said, finally understanding why I recognized her. "Warden... Morda?"

She smiled brilliantly. While she wasn't all that attractive of a woman—too thin, not soft enough. Too small. At least for me, and my beast. We favored curvy and lush.

We *only* favored Gabriela.

A *warden* of the Interstellar Brides Program was my mate?

Warden Morda smiled—the smile made her look so much different. Happy. "That's right. I'm pleased you remembered. You helped me once, at the guard gate."

I did remember, although vaguely. I'd helped so many people, volunteers to both the Brides Program and the Coalition Fleet. She didn't stand out for me, but I didn't dare say that now.

Rachel glanced from me, to Wendy, and back. When she realized I had nothing more to say, she kept talking, filling the empty space, waiting for the governor to get his ass back over here and *fix this.* "If you were a warden at the Interstellar Brides Processing Center, how did you end up here?"

Wendy shrugged, her shy look returning. Too meek. I could not imagine her riding my cock, screaming my name, begging me for more—as Gabriela had done last night.

"I don't know. I've matched so many brides, you know? I don't have family, at least none that I keep up with. No pets to leave behind or anything like that. I thought, why not? Why not find my own perfect mate? So many women got their *One* and I wanted my own turn. So here I am, matched to you. They told me the match was ninety-nine percent." Her gaze shifted to me and her face turned a deep shade of pink. "That means we should be perfect for each other, in all ways, right?"

Behind me, Gabriela made a gasping sound. Wendy ignored her. Completely. Her intense focus shifted solely to me. Then to Jori. "You... you are holding a baby."

I'd forgotten about him, but pride coursed through me, and I patted his back again. "Yes, he is mine."

Her eyes widened. "You... you have a *baby?*"

"Yes, with Gabriela." I turned to indicate my mate. She stood by the door, arms folded over her chest. She looked... small. Wary. It was obvious she wasn't excited about Warden Morda... Wendy, being here. Neither was I. The sooner this was resolved, the sooner she and I could leave.

"But... but... what is she doing here?"

Wendy asked. "*I'm* your mate. We've been matched."

The governor joined us and I looked at him, hoping for a quick resolution. He offered none. "She is correct. I confirmed in the Interstellar Brides' records. Wendy Morda *is* your match. There has been no mistake in transport. The testing data shows a nearly perfect match." He tilted his head toward Wendy, who was looking at me.

"It's okay if you have a baby," she told me. "I always wanted to be a mother. I can help you take care of him."

Was she insane? "I don't need help, Wendy. He already has a mother. There's been a mistake."

Wendy walked toward me, and I had no idea how to handle her obviously tender feelings without destroying her. I knew Gabriela, knew just how fragile a human female's heart could be. I didn't want to hurt Wendy—but she wasn't mine. Would never be mine.

My mate appeared at my side. I hadn't

heard her approach. "Here, I'll take him," Gabriella practically whispered, holding her hands out for Jori.

Wendy stepped closer. "No, it's fine," she said, as if she had some say over what we did with our baby. "I had thought we'd have to wait... about nine months to have a baby. But this is better. Not only do I have a mate, but a child, too."

She looked so earnest, so eager. I felt... nothing. Distaste, perhaps. She thought we'd have a baby in nine months? That meant... fuck, that meant she wanted to start right away. Like now. And she was prepared to make Jori hers?

No fucking way.

"Jorik," Gabriela whispered, interrupting my thoughts. "Please."

I handed her Jori, but I said to Wendy, "There has been a mistake. I'm sorry. I already have a mate. Gabriela is my mate."

Wendy glanced at Gabriela, then me. "You're not wearing mating cuffs. If she were your mate, wouldn't she be cuffed?"

Gabriela froze, her gaze lifting to mine

with a look I did not like. Suspicion? Accusation? Doubt?

Pain?

Fuck. What Wendy said was true. I hadn't mentioned the mating cuffs to Gabriela because they were not here. I wanted to surprise her when they arrived from Atlan. I wanted to get on my knees and offer myself to her, allow her to place the cuffs on my wrists and claim me for her own.

I wanted that moment. My beast demanded it. I had requested the cuffs be transported from my home planet, but had not considered that the slight delay would cause a problem. Gabriela was mine. I was hers. I needed no visible proof other than Jori.

Until I did. Like now.

"Jorik?" Gabriela asked, her voice full of question.

I turned to her, took in the look on her face. Her smile was gone. Her... life. Vitality. It was as if the arrival of Wendy had sucked it from her. Bled her of it. Jori started to fuss and she swayed and patted his back. "He's hungry. I have to feed him."

"I'll go with you," I said, wanting to be anywhere but here, anywhere but with *her*.

And *only* with Gabriela. How dare this human take my time away from my true mate!

"Wait!" Wendy said. "What about me?"

I glanced at her, then back at Gabriela.

"Go," Gabriela said softly. "She's your matched mate."

"But—"

Gabriela fiercely shook her head. "Go. You need to take care of her. Of this." She swung her hand through the air, encompassing the entire room. Wendy. The transport pad. This cluster-fuck. I turned and the door opened silently behind me. Gabriela took Jori and fled. By the gods, I wished I could join her. My heart went with her, and I wanted to follow with a desperation that made my beast howl.

I looked at the governor, who shrugged. "I'll send an inquiry to Earth. Not sure what to do. I've never heard of this happening before. I need to contact Prillon Prime to find out proper protocol."

I was glad to know that even he could see Gabriela was my true mate. That Wendy, regardless of what the testing said, was *not*. It eased my misery, a little, knowing he doubted as well.

"How long will that take?" I asked, desperate to get away from Wendy, back to Gabriela. But I was not a cruel male. This poor female had traveled across the galaxy, expecting to be mine. Eager to be mine.

It wasn't her fault I did not want her. I could be courteous, at least. Offer her my protection until a new mate was chosen for her. Technically, right now, she was mine. My responsibility.

A small hand took mine. I looked down. Wendy. She looked up at me, smiled. "There's nothing to worry about.

You'll see. I'm so glad I'm here, mate. We will be so happy together."

She went up on her tiptoes to try and kiss me. Thank fuck she was so small and she barely got her mouth near my shoulder.

I stepped back, held out my hands to ward her off just like I had all the warriors wanting to touch Jori in the cafeteria. They'd been eager, but sweet. This? Wendy Morda trying to kiss me?

I was revolted. My beast couldn't handle it.

It was like, with that failed attempt at intimacy, everything I'd just said to her about already having a mate, about Gabriela, meant nothing. Was she confused? Ill? Or did she simply not care?

Fuck.

13

*J*orik

"THIS ISN'T YOUR QUARTERS," she said as I let her precede me into the room. She looked about, frowned.

I took in the plain space. White walls, dark flooring. A small bed, not sized for an Atlan and especially not two Prillons with their mate. A table, chair and S-Gen machine. I knew a bathing room was through the door on the left.

"No. This is for guests."

Those who aren't staying.

She turned and looked up at me. "I thought we'd be going to your rooms." She stepped close and ran her hand up my chest. "To... get to know each other."

Her smile was pure seduction, but it made me step back, bump into the wall. Gods, this slip of a female had me on the retreat. Even the Hive hadn't done that.

My beast growled for her to stay away, but it had the opposite effect on her. She stepped closer, so close I felt the press of her breasts against my belly. Her leg settled between mine so her pussy rubbed up against my thigh. I could feel her heat, the tight points of her nipples.

I clenched my hands into fists, not to keep from touching her, but to keep from tossing her across the room. She was bold, forward. Brazen.

"Wendy," I said through clenched teeth.

When she put her palm against my cock, she frowned, looked up at me. "You're big, but not hard." Then she grinned. "I know just the way to change that."

She licked her lips, her little fingers beginning to work open my uniform pants.

"I wonder if Atlans like a good cock sucking. I've been told I'm really good at it. Like a Hoover."

I didn't know what a Hoover was, but it sounded as if she'd done this often and I did not wish to be in a long line of many.

"And don't worry, I swallow. Every drop." She winked. "Mate."

Fuck, no. The word *mate* broke me from my fear. Yes, I was actually a little afraid of this human. I didn't think she'd hurt me physically, but she was aggressive and wild. Too wild. And I didn't want to dishonor myself by hurting her.

I didn't want her to suck my cock. I didn't want her to have a single drop of my seed. That was all for Gabriela.

Gabriela.

I thought of her right now, alone. With Jori. My family was elsewhere on the base, and I was about to have my cock sucked by another female.

"No," I growled, taking hold of her shoulders. "I don't want a Hoover. I want Gabriela. She is my mate. *You* are not. There has been a mistake. I don't know why. I don't know how."

She looked up at me, horrified, then she crumbled. Tears filled her eyes, her shoulders drooped. "You don't want me?"

I didn't say anything because I'd just made that clear.

"It's because of her? I can give you everything she can. And more. She's just had a baby. Stretch marks. Sagging boobs. Extra weight." She ran a hand over her hip. "Don't you want a younger model? Someone fit. Taut. I can do things she can't."

"Gabriela is the mother of my son. She is my mate. I'm sorry, Wendy. I cannot give you what you want."

"But *I'm* your matched mate." She pleaded, running her hands over my body, then reaching up to cup my face in her hands. "I'm prettier, Jorik. And I love you more than she does. I can give you children. Lots of them. I will be a good mother. You'll see." She leaned forward, pressed her lips to my uniform where it covered my chest.

Prettier? No. Wendy's face was a raptor's face, more like a Prillon's than my sweet Gabriela with her soft, round cheeks and full lips. Everything about my mate was soft and welcoming, feminine and beautiful.

She dared claim to be superior to Gabriela? She'd pointed out so many things about my mate, listing them as if they were flaws, when in fact they were all attributes. She'd just had *my* baby. The little red lines on her belly were proof she'd been round with *my* child, giving it shelter. And she had no sagging boobs—if the English slang meant what I assumed—as they were full, heavy and very sensitive. The extra weight was perfect. She'd been too thin before, at least for me. Now I had curves to grip, to caress, to sink into. She was just as I desired.

And this female? Wendy Morda? She was trim and toned, but bony. And worse, her personality grated on me, tortured me worse than the Hive. For when I'd been taunted by them, I'd had hope that Gabriela would someday be mine.

Now, Wendy was the one taking her away from me. I wouldn't have it.

I grabbed her wrists and lowered them from my face. Gently, controlling my strength, I pushed her away. "I already have a mate, Wendy. Choose another."

"I don't want anyone else, Jorik. I want you. It's always been you."

I turned on my heel, waved the door open and stalked out, leaving her behind. It was rude, but I didn't care. If I remained, soon enough, she'd be climbing me like an Atlan tree.

When I arrived at the Command Center, I went right up to Governor Rone, interrupted his conversation with Kiel, the Everian Hunter, and got in his face.

"That human is *not* my mate," I shouted, pointing at the door that had slid closed. "She scares the shit out of me."

The governor began to smile, but stifled it.

"The only female I want touching my cock is Gabriela. I don't care if it's a one hundred percent match through the testing. Wendy. Morda. Is. Not. My. Mate."

Kiel seemed to be smart enough to walk away, knowing whatever he was sharing with the governor, even if it were the Hive invading, it wasn't as important as this.

"Get me Warden Egara on the comms. Now," the governor ordered.

I stood beside him, faced the large comms screen on the wall. It took less than a minute, but a female with dark hair and a kind face filled the display. I'd met her before during my time on Earth. All my interactions had been on the Coalition side; I'd had no contact within the grounds with the Brides Center other then with the Wardens. They were free to come and go anywhere on the grounds, and often could be found on the fighter side, coordinating with the representative of the Fleet.

"Governor, it's good to see your face. I hope Rachel is well."

I knew Rachel had been matched through the Brides Center, and it was thoughtful of her to ask, although I didn't really give a shit.

I stepped forward so her attention was on me. "Warden, I've been matched to a female."

She smiled brilliantly and it changed her whole face. She was quite pretty. "Yes, how are Gabriela and your little baby? Congratulations, by the way."

"Thank you. They are well. But I am not speaking of Gabriela. I am referring to the female I was matched to through the Brides Center."

She frowned. "Gabriela is your mate, Warlord. I transported her and your son to you there on The Colony personally."

My beast growled in frustration.

"Warden, he is referring to the testing that he did the other day," the governor added. "A match has been made and she transported here earlier."

"That's not possible. What is her name?"

"Wendy Morda," he told her.

Her eyes widened. "Let me check," she said.

I held my breath as she looked down, presumably working one of the tablets I knew was in use at the facility there on Earth.

"Holy shit," she whispered. When she looked back at us, her eyes were wide and she looked a little stunned.

"What is it, Warden?" I asked, trying to remain calm.

"Are you telling me Wendy Morda is there on The Colony? Now?"

I shuddered, thinking of her hand on my cock. "Yes," I said. "And she is adamant she is my mate."

"The testing data shows a successful match," the governor added.

"Yes, the data does show that," she confirmed. "However, she was not successfully tested. There is no record of her ever volunteering. She is not your match."

I sighed in relief. *Thank the gods.*

"Then how is it she is listed that way in the system?" the governor asked.

"I don't know. She has access to the system, to the data. I believe she falsified the records and matched herself to Jorik."

Fury filled me, every drop of blood in my body filling with rage as the day of my escape and rescue—the day Captain Mills had contacted Earth—came to mind. "And the day I contacted you, Warden, and you told me Gabriela had married another male? The day you lied to me and told me nothing of my son?"

"What?" The warden looked genuinely confused and I sighed in relief, even as my beast fought to emerge and rip the room to pieces. The warden had not been involved in the deception. That much was obvious. And she was the one who had matched Rachel to the governor, sent the other brides, sent Gabriela and my son to me. I could forgive her, but not the one who had denied me my mate and my bride. "When was this?"

"The day a ReCon team picked us up from Latiri 4, I contacted Earth, Miami, the brides' center, and asked about my mate. I was told she had presumed me dead and married a human male."

"Just a moment." Glaring at her screen, the warden's fingers raced over her controls. "Damn it. There's no record of that comm. No record at all." Her skin became flushed, bright red and her eyes sparkled with fury. "I will get to the bottom of this, but I have a feeling I already know exactly what happened."

"Is this normal procedure on Earth? To lie to the warriors waiting for a bride? To deceive us?" I wondered, suddenly worried for every male in the Coalition Fleet. The warriors fought and died to protect the Coalition worlds. To have their ultimate gift, their bride, be sent based on lies? The thought sickened me.

"God, no." The warden looked sad for a moment, then glanced down again at her tablet. "I should have done more to monitor her. This is my responsibility. I don't normally share personal data, but Wendy Morda's file was flagged, Governor. She tested to become a bride, several times, but not successfully. Her testing has never been completed. Each time, the test ended abruptly. She failed the psychological profile necessary to receive a match as a bride."

"How do you fail testing?" I asked. "I didn't want to do it, but I just sat there and went to sleep for a bit. Dreamed."

She nodded. "Yes, but that is because you are stable."

I frowned. "I came from months of torture at the hands of the Hive. You call that stable?"

"In comparison to Warden Morda, yes." She sighed and set her tablet aside. "I suspect she became obsessed with you during your time here on Earth, Warlord. When you contacted Earth, I suspect it was Wendy who received the comm—and lied to you about your mate and your son so she could falsify her match to you." The warden rubbed her forehead with her fingertips, as if her head were aching. "I suspect, Jorik, that she did what she did because she wanted you for herself."

I shuddered, thinking of what might have been. Though I'd been crushed, I'd accepted what I'd been told. I'd assumed Gabriela was living out the rest of her days with her human mate. If Gabriela had arrived a single day later, it would have been too late. I would have trusted that the brides' testing was accurate, tried to make Wendy Morda—and my beast— happy. I would have accepted my new bride with honor and tried to love her.

The thought chilled me to my very core.

The governor took a step forward and his hands were clenched into fists. I was not the only one upset by this news. "And you allowed her to remain in her position at the testing center?" the governor asked.

"She is perfectly capable of running our computer programs, Governor. However, failing the testing *should* have locked her out of the testing protocols, kept her here, on Earth."

He crossed his arms over his chest. "She's *not* on Earth. She's here."

"And she wants me," I added.

"I would consider her mentally unstable, Governor," Warden Egara said. "Please take her into custody and send her back to me as soon as possible."

"I will find her, Warden, but she broke Coalition law, not Earth's. When I find her, she'll go to Prillon Prime, to a Fleet brig. Prime Nial can decide what to do with her," he replied, clapping me on the back. Hard. My beast welcomed the contact, the reassurance that everything was going to be fine. Gabriela was mine. Wendy would go to Prillon Prime and face the consequences of her actions.

"I'll go get her. She's not going to resist me," I added. "She wants me, perhaps too eagerly. I made it clear, directly upon her transport, that Gabriela was my mate, that there had been a mistake. I also made it clear after I took her to the guest quarters. Wendy knows I do not want the match."

"She knows about Gabriela and the baby?" she asked.

I nodded. "Yes, she met both of them upon her arrival, then assured me that she still wanted me, that we had an instant family and she would be happy to care for Jori."

The warden stood abruptly. "Where is she now?"

I looked to the governor whose shoulders had gone stiff.

"I left her in the guest quarters."

"You would be in no danger, Warlord," Warden Egara said. "But Gabriela could be. From what I've learned today, I would say Wendy is disturbed enough to believe that if she gets rid of Gabriela, she can become your mate and Jori's mother."

"Illogical. That would never be the case, Warden. Neither I, nor my beast, would ever accept her."

The warden's look was grim. "This isn't about logic, Jorik. It's about obsession."

The governor's gaze met mine, and the worry I saw there intensified my own. "Where is Gabriela? And your son?"

I looked at my bare wrists, the cuffs that would have kept Gabriela safe—and close—noticeably absent. My unadorned skin made a mockery of what I'd promised my female. Love. Protection. Safety. "I don't know."

I don't know.

Some amazing fucking mate I was turning out to be. I'd allowed Gabriela to walk away from me without a thought to where she would go. I'd walked with the liar, the traitor, the female who might intend to hurt my mate, and allowed her to put her hands on me. Talk to me. Make her claim on me. Yes, I'd rejected her, but I had not gone to my mate. I'd come here. To the governor, and left my mate unprotected.

The governor turned to his comm officer. "Call in Kiel and that Hunter's unit. I need his tracking ability. And send word to every watch station. We need to find these females. Now."

"Yes, sir." The Prillon warrior nodded, his gaze darted to me. Away. Quickly. But I saw what he didn't want me to see anyway.

Sorrow. And pity. As if my mate and son were already lost.

Fuck.

14

*G*abriela

I STOOD LOOKING DOWN at my son, tears streaking my cheeks. I was exhausted. Between the transport, sexual gymnastics, taking care of Jori's—and Jorik's—needs, I was beyond tired.

But that was just physical and taking Rachel up on babysitting and getting a nap would help with that.

But mentally, I was a wreck. What was I going to do? Jorik had a matched mate, a woman who had been selected to be perfect for him in every way.

Who was I? I didn't want to be the woman who trapped a man with a baby he never wanted in the first place. Sure, he wanted Jori now, and I didn't want to leave him.

Less than a day ago, everything had been perfect. And now?

Now, I was the third wheel on a planet where I didn't belong. Now, Jorik had an Earth woman who was chosen for him. If I tried to keep him for myself, I'd be stealing that potential happiness from both Jorik and Wendy.

They were matched with almost perfect certainty. How could I argue with that proof?

She seemed nice enough. Shy. Small. Much thinner than I was. Younger.

God. What the hell was I even thinking?

"Sleep, little guy. I promise we'll be okay." I leaned over and kissed Jori on his precious face. He looked more like his father every day. Like an Atlan. Jorik's coloring. His jaw. His nose. And those eyes? Either one of my guys would just stare at me and I melted.

Leaving Jori to his nap, I closed the bedroom door, made sure the sound monitor was on—Jorik had shown me how late last night when I couldn't sleep with worry—and went into the living area. The couch looked too soft. Too comfortable for the restlessness I was feeling right now.

I'd fed Jori. Changed him. Played with him. Kissed him. Rocked him. I'd done everything I could think of to keep my mind off Jorik and Wendy, alone. Talking. Somewhere. Maybe *more* than talking.

Was he falling in love with her right now? Was he looking at her and thinking —*Hey, she's beautiful. Maybe I made a mistake?*

I sat down at the small table in a kitchenette area and placed my arms on the table, stared at my bare wrists.

Was there a reason he hadn't offered me the mating cuffs?

"Of course, there was a reason, idiot." I just didn't want to say that reason out loud. Didn't even want to think the words, but they were there, in the back of my mind. Spoken or not, the truth was the truth. Jorik had never offered me his cuffs because—well, he just had chosen not to. I was not going to be the woman waiting around for years, longing for a diamond ring and a marriage proposal. Even if we had a baby together, it seemed I wasn't going to be anything more to him than just a baby mama.

The Atlan, Rezzer, wore his cuffs proudly. As did his mate, CJ. Although I'd been told to call her Caroline now, so she would not be confused with her daughter. Little CJ and RJ. The twins. The oddness of their name choice made me smile— and wish things were like they had been yesterday. When I was happy, deliriously happy, and completely ignorant of the truth.

I was *not* Jorik's match. I was not meant to be his mate. Our meeting, my trip here? All a big mistake. No, Jori belonged here. As his mother, I did as well, but not with Jorik.

Sure, I loved him. Too much. I loved him enough to let him go.

The baby shifted, making a cooing noise and I wiped a tear from my cheek. Jori would visit his father. I'd make sure of that. He deserved to know Jorik, and the Atlan loved his son. He had Atlan things to teach him I knew nothing about. Unusual customs he would need to know. He was big and would be huge like his father. He needed Jorik's guidance.

But I couldn't stay here and watch him fall in love with another woman, remain calm as months went by and Jorik realized he'd made a terrible mistake.

Honor would keep him by my side. I

knew that. He was a good male. He would not abandon the mother of his son.

But he could grow to resent me, see me as an obligation rather than a blessing.

I'd been with him—really with him—for less than two days. How could he possibly have real, lasting feelings for me after such a short time?

"The same way I love him." I was talking to myself, but it wouldn't help. I had never been lucky. Not with family, or relationships, or love. To think that would suddenly change was foolish, and I'd learned very early in life not to trust in foolish fantasies. And that's what this was —a fantasy. A dream.

And now it was time to wake up and go back to work. I had a son to raise.

I hadn't brought much with me, the ratty sweats and T-shirt I'd had on and Jori's baby blanket. I used the S-Gen machine to make a medium sized purse and stuffed it full of Jori's things because that outfit from Earth wasn't making a round trip. I'd take my son, find the transport room and go back to Miami. To reality. Jorik could visit him there.

Warden Egara could take care of visitation rights. I wasn't sure how that would work, or if they'd even take Jori back on Earth. I'd say I had extenuating circumstances, especially since the warden had been the one to get me here in the first place. Surely, she'd understand. But if not, I guess I would have to figure out something on Atlan.

The one thing I knew for certain was that I couldn't remain here, on The Colony, and watch Jorik love someone else.

I was strong. I'd had to be, but that would break me. And Jori needed a strong mother, not a broken one.

I was done crying when a light knock sounded on the door. Jorik would have simply marched in, so I knew I had a visitor. And from the tentative nature of the knock, I was guessing a woman. Maybe Rachel? Come to commiserate with me?

Or try to convince me that everything was going to be fine?

Using my palm, I unlocked the door as I'd seen Jorik do, shocked to find Wendy staring back at me. We were of similar height, the blue Atlan gown she wore a nearly identical match to mine. The moment was surreal, as if I was staring at a new, younger, thinner version of myself.

She was too pale, her hair a lighter brown, not the gorgeous black I'd always been a bit proud of, but she wasn't horribly unattractive. I tried not to hate her, but I nearly choked on the feeling despite my best efforts. "Wendy. What a surprise."

Where was Jorik?

Wendy shrugged apologetically, a half smile on her face. "Hi. I was wondering if we could talk?"

That was the *last* thing in the world I wanted, but I nodded my head and stepped back so she could come into the room.

She didn't budge, her gaze going to the purse I'd placed next to the door.

"Can we go for a walk? I don't want to be rude, but I don't want Jorik to walk in on us."

Well, that, at least, I could agree with. If I was a blubbering mess, he didn't need to see that. And if I wanted to strangle Wendy where she stood, I didn't want him to see that either.

Hell, maybe I'd just sit on the skinny bitch so she couldn't breathe.

"Jori is napping. I can't leave him."

Wendy smiled. "Yes, I thought of that."

The Warlord, Kai, stepped into view. He smiled at me reassuringly. "I can watch him for you. I'll protect him with my life. You have my word."

I trusted the Atlan, knew he would, literally, die to protect Jorik's son, so I nodded and stepped into the hallway. "You are my first babysitter, ever. Don't tell Rachel."

He nodded as if he'd been given the gravest of missions, and no doubt understood Rachel would be angry if she discovered she hadn't gotten first dibs. "I just fed him and he's sleeping. I should be back before he wakes up."

Kai smiled. "I was nearly fifteen when my mother gave birth to my younger sister. I have experience with babies."

That was interesting to know. "Okay." And I did want to talk to Wendy. Alone. "Thanks."

He nodded and I walked out into the hallway, the door sliding closed behind me. Wendy followed, and when I turned to ask where she wished to go, I spotted the strap of my purse over her shoulder. I thought to say something, but then decided not to bother. She was obviously trying to be nice. Purses were a totally normal thing on Earth, and most women didn't leave their house without one.

Whatever. She could be my pack mule. That was the only satisfaction I was going to get from this hellish, heartbreaking day. And if my emotions didn't stop swinging like a monster-sized pendulum, I was going to have a complete mental breakdown before I made it back to Earth. Maybe I needed to go back into a ReGen pod for a little while. A little "me" time.

"Kai took me on a tour," she said. "The base is really quite lovely, don't you think?"

I hadn't seen most of it yet, only what I'd seen out the big windows of the cafeteria. I'd been too busy having orgasms to care what the rest of the base looked like. I nodded in mute agreement and kept walking as Wendy led us from hallway to hallway, past a large garden area that had some plants I actually recognized. "It that a rose bush?" I wondered.

"Oh, yes. I guess when Rachel first arrived, she didn't like how sparse everything was. She started importing plants from all over the place. All different planets. Kai showed me some lovely purple and green flowers from Atlan. I can't wait to visit there."

Wow, she'd learned a lot in a short time. I'd been here longer, and I knew none of that. Then again, I'd been busy having beast sex with Jorik. Maybe that meant... no, I wouldn't even go there, thinking of Jorik and Wendy having sex.

"Yes. That would be nice," I replied neutrally. Or not, if I was banished there with my alien son. But I'd deal. I knew for a fact that Atlans liked ice cream.

Wendy's voice had a singsong quality to it. "Yes. I have imagined it many times. I'll be with Jorik"—she glanced at me from under her lashes—"and of course, his son. We'll have two or three more children no doubt because he's so virile. All of them big and strong, like their father."

I should have said something kind, something *nice,* but I couldn't choke the words past my lips. So I said nothing.

We'd passed the garden and had gone down another very long hallway. There was no one here, and when the corridor ended, we were in some kind of storage room. Large boxes lined the walls, storage containers marked with transport codes like the ones I'd seen in the room when I first arrived. I had no idea what was in them. Didn't care.

I turned and faced her, crossed my arms over my chest. "What are we doing here, Wendy? And what did you want to talk to me about?" If I didn't weigh double what the other woman did, I might have been afraid. As it was, I was impatient. Irritated.

"I wanted to talk to you about Jorik."

Yeah, duh. "So talk."

"And Jori."

That got my hackles up. "Jori is not up for discussion."

She was wringing her hands in front of her stomach, pacing. Agitated. She looked... desperate. "I want you to know that I love Jorik. I've loved him for a long time."

I frowned. A long time? She'd only been on the planet a few hours at most. She'd said they'd met on Earth, but Jorik had barely recognized her. "How is that possible?"

"I told you—everyone in the transport

room—I worked with him at the Bride Processing Center. When I decided to become a bride—well, I was beyond thrilled to hear I was matched to Jorik. It was perfect."

I'd just bet it was. Bitch.

When I said nothing, she continued moving, walking around me in circles, so I had to constantly turn to keep her in front of me. "He's so tall and kind and brave. And I know his son will be just like him. I already love Jori, too." She stopped pacing and smiled at me, her eyes glassy with tears. "He's such a beautiful baby."

She'd seen him for about two minutes. Total.

"Yes, he is."

"I want you to know that I will love him like he's my own. I'll take care of him. I promise you that."

I frowned. As her own? "What?" Had I heard her correctly? "He's *my* son. I'm taking him back to Earth."

Her eyes teared and she shook her

head. "Oh, no. Jorik won't like that. He'll be sad."

Yes, he would. "He can visit."

"But Jori is my son," she said, her voice taking on a whine. "You can't take him to Earth. He won't love me if you take him away from his mother."

I put my hand to my chest. "I'm his mother." It was time to get the hell out of here. This bitch was crazy. I had to warn Jorik. "I'm done here." I spun on my heel to leave, but I was too late. Wendy dashed between me and the door, her long dress wrapping around her legs as she did so.

When she pulled the ion blaster from a side pocket, I froze.

Shit. Slowly, I raised my hands.

"You are done," she said, her voice flat. "You are right about that. Jorik loves you. He told me he couldn't be with me. That he loves you and his son." She lifted the blaster and motioned for me to move to my right, toward one of the storage containers. I shuffled in the direction she wanted, never taking my eyes off her. We were alone. No one was coming to my rescue. Jori was safe, but even Kai didn't know where we'd gone.

And this crazy bitch was not getting her hands on my son. Or Jorik. Who loved me. He'd told her he loved me. Couldn't be with her. Didn't *want* her.

I'd never wanted to laugh and scream at the same time, until now. My heart beat so hard it pounded in my ears.

Wendy lifted the weapon, her eyes a little wild. "Get into that transport crate. I don't want to kill you, I'm a mother now, not a murderer, but you have to go away. Jorik won't love me if you're here. Jori won't love me if you're here. You have to go."

I don't want to kill you. But she would. I could see it in the glazed fanaticism in her gaze. She'd obviously been obsessed with Jorik when he worked at the Brides' center on Earth. Obsessed enough to follow him into space, to another world. To match herself to him with a fake test.

Insane enough to think that if she

killed me, he would love her. My son would love her. That if I disappeared, she would just step right into place. That Jorik or anyone else on The Colony would just shrug and be fine with me disappearing and Wendy holding my son.

My son.

She was trying to steal my family.

Walking away to give Jorik a chance at happiness with a true matched mate was one thing.

This? This was wrong. This filled my blood with fire. This woman was threatening my child. My man. My *family.*

If she twitched, I was going to take her down. People didn't fuck with an Atlan beast. Everyone knew that. But a woman whose baby was being threatened? Oh, yeah. Wendy was going down.

Moving carefully, I lifted one leg over the open crate, then the other until I stood, facing her, the crate hitting me at my waist. It was like standing in a huge, empty box.

"You aren't right for him," she

snapped. "You know that." Wendy lifted the blaster, aimed at my chest. "I'm doing this for Jorik. You'll see. He's going to love me."

I shook my head. "No, Wendy. He won't. Even if you kill me. Even if I'm out of the picture. He'll never make a family with you. *I'm* his family."

She shrieked, the crazy showing in the glassy sheen of her eyes and the snarl on her lips. I shouldn't have taunted her.

She pulled the trigger and a sharp blast of light exploded in my chest.

I fell, collapsing inside the crate. I struggled to draw air into my lungs as the lid was placed over me, pounded into place. Darkness pressed heavily.

There was a jostling motion and I could hear Wendy mumbling as the movement came to an abrupt halt. The crate was dropped, my body with it, but the additional pain was like a flea bite compared to the burning in my chest. Wendy's voice came through the lid.

"I'm going to send you away, somewhere they'll never, ever find you." She pounded on the lid, hissed at me like a snake. "Jorik is mine."

Fuck. Fuck. Fuck.

I forced air into my lungs, ignored the burn. Ignored the wave of nausea that made me gag as I rolled onto my back and pulled my knees toward my chest. My head spun, the pain worse than any migraine I'd ever had as I lifted my feet, wishing I had on combat boots like Jorik wore and not pretty blue slippers.

It didn't matter. I'd pound my feet into bloody splinters if it meant getting out of this crate and saving my son.

Jorik? He was a Warlord. He was fierce and brave and strong.

But Jori? My baby? He was innocent. Small. Fragile.

I was going to kill this fucking bitch with my bare hands.

Using every ounce of strength I could muster, I kicked up at the lid of the crate.

Electricity built in the air around me. Oh shit, I knew what that meant. The transport pad had been turned on. It was powering up to send me god only knew where. Probably into the middle of deep space where I'd die in seconds. All so this bitch could try to steal my family. And she could do it, too. She'd transported herself here from Earth.

Closing my eyes, I kicked again. Again. Again. I had to get out. Save my family.

The power level rose, the hair on my head rising to cling to my face like a blanket of static.

Kick.

The lid cracked, a thin strip of light poured in.

I kicked again, screaming as I heard her mumbling frantically to herself. Seemed the transport wasn't working properly.

Thank god. Or Jorik's gods. Or blind damn luck.

I kicked the lid off and stood on shaky legs, forcing my pain-filled head to focus on my enemy. The woman who wanted to steal my baby. My life.

She glanced up, her eyes wide, frantic. "No! No!" Her hands moved faster over the transport control panel.

I climbed out of the crate. Took one wobbly step.

The door opened and Jorik rushed in with Wulf, Egon, Braun and the governor. They were all armed, blasters pointing at Wendy. With a precision I didn't quite believe, Wulf took aim and shot the blaster from Wendy's hand. It flew, landing too far from her to be a threat.

She screamed, then burst into tears. "No, Jorik. I love you. We'll be so happy together! Don't you understand? I'm doing this for you. For us."

He looked at me and apparently didn't like what he saw. His beast burst free from one second to the next. Huge. Fierce. Enraged. "No. Gabriela. My mate. Mine."

His words made my entire body sing. He did love me. Want me. Not her.

Not. Her.

"No, I'm your mate," she continued. "Jorik. Listen. Me. I'm your matched mate." She pushed something again on the panel, waved her arms over the transport controls. Glanced at me.

"That's not going to work." The governor's deep voice sounded... resigned. "All transport has been locked down."

"No!" Wendy screamed again. "No. Jorik is mine."

Jorik took a step toward her, and I recognized the killing rage I'd only seen once before in the ice cream shop right before he'd ripped that man's head off.

Wendy wasn't a man. She was mentally ill, but she wasn't a warrior.

I didn't need Jorik to take care of this for me.

And I was closer.

I lifted a hand to stop him. "No, Jorik." Three more steps and Wendy looked into my eyes with fear.

"I love him," she whispered. Was that supposed to be an apology?

"He's mine," I snarled. "And so is Jori." The rage boiled over, and I did something I had never done in my life. I hit her so hard I knocked her to the ground in one punch.

Seeing her fall didn't calm me. Rage exploded through every cell of my body. I felt like a beast. She'd threatened my son. My baby.

I stood over her, then dropped to my knees straddling her. I lifted my fist to pound her into dust, but huge Atlan arms wrapped around me.

Jorik.

"Mate. No. Hurt hands."

That made me burst out laughing. Of all the insane, ridiculous things he could say to me right now. He didn't care if I punched the woman, only that I would bruise my hands?

Once I turned into Jorik's arms, I clung to my mate, held on for dear life to the only thing that made sense right now, Wulf and Egon moved past me to take care of Wendy. "Jori?" I asked.

Wulf turned to me. "He's safe with Kai, who wants to beat himself bloody for letting you leave with her." Wulf lifted

Wendy to her feet and the poor woman didn't protest. She looked, broken, and so did her nose. Blood dripped down her face and she'd definitely have a black eye.

Take that, bitch.

Despite that, I couldn't quite bring myself to feel sorry for her.

"Take her to the brig," the governor ordered. "Lock her up. I'll have to file this with CFPC Command on Prillon Prime."

"Not Earth?" I asked.

The governor looked at me. "She didn't break Earth's laws, she broke ours."

Oh, shit. I hadn't even thought of that. The Interstellar Brides' Program was important to the Coalition. Very, very important.

Governor Maxim shook his head. "Wendy not only abused the system, she lied to Jorik about his mate and son, falsified her match, and tried to kidnap an Atlan's mate. She'll be in a Coalition prison for a very long time."

They took Wendy away and I didn't

move, needing to feel my Atlan's arms around me.

"Mine." Jorik's beast held me like I was precious glass. So gently.

I held him tighter. "I love you, Jorik."

We stood that way for a very long time, and I was okay with that.

15

G abriela

"As they say on Earth, I'm not messing around," I told Wulf, who stood beside me in the transport room. We were looking at the transport pad, waiting for the mating cuffs I had discovered my mate ordered from Atlan the day I arrived.

The day I arrived. All my worry about not being his chosen mate, about the darn mating cuffs could have been avoided if he'd just *told me.*

His hand was poised above the touch screen, and he looked down at me. "I don't think you want to create messes around other males. Jorik will not be pleased if you wish to spend time with other males."

He looked so serious I had to laugh.

"What?" he wondered, frowning.

"Jorik is the only male I want. And Jori is more than messy enough for me."

His broad shoulders relaxed. We'd been through enough already, and I was sure he was relieved everything was all happily ever after.

I was, too. Jorik—holding Jori snug in his arms—was with the governor talking with Warden Egara. I wanted no part of that, so I'd tugged Wulf with me for this important task.

"What I meant was, I want mating cuffs on Jorik. I don't want any other lunatic showing up and trying to take him away from me."

"Ah," he said. "Yes, considering what

you've been through, that is reasonable, but shouldn't Jorik be putting them on you?"

"Like I said, I'm not taking any chances," I replied. "I want those on his wrists as soon as possible."

"You know there's more to an Atlan claiming than just putting the mating cuffs on."

I nodded. "I'm getting the cuffs. Jorik, I'm sure, can take charge of the rest."

I bit my lip, trying not to smile as I thought of Jorik taking charge. I liked when he was all wild and beast-like in bed... or out. And this... claiming? I was wet just thinking about it.

Wulf grunted and went back to pushing buttons. "Ordering such elaborate cuffs isn't usual, but neither is anything about your match."

I frowned. "What do you mean?"

Wulf grinned. "Jorik has no more males in his family line. No one to pass on a pair of mating cuffs. Usually, we are gifted cuffs from our grandfathers, or great-grandfathers when they die. Most mating cuffs are hundreds of years old."

"But?" This was intriguing, and I was a bit sad to know that Jorik didn't have any family. But he did. He had me and Jori, and I was never leaving him. They'd have to pry my cold, dead fingers off his body after I died. Even then, I'd probably come back and haunt whoever forced me to leave him.

"Jorik created a new family design. The cuffs were ordered from the most talented craftsman on Atlan. They are worth more than most Atlan estates."

Holy shit. "Seriously?" So much for a big diamond ring. This sounded like so much more. "Like a house?"

Wulf grunted. "No. Like a castle and lands." He grinned as the transport pad hummed, the *very* familiar electrical pull making my hair raise. "Your mate is extremely wealthy, as all Atlan warriors are."

That confused me, but I couldn't take my eyes off the gorgeous box that appeared in the middle of the transport pad.

Decorated with intricate carvings, I couldn't even imagine how beautiful the cuffs must be to come in a box like that. "If you're all so rich, why do you live here?"

He frowned. "We are not welcome on Atlan. We pose too great a risk to our people." He sounded sad, a bit lost, so I let it drop. I'd ask Jorik later.

Wulf walked to the platform, picked up the box like it weighed no more than a shoebox—even though it was obviously heavy metal and very solid—and placed it at my feet. He flipped a latch and lifted the lid.

I glanced down.

"Wow." Large multi-colored wrist cuffs lay nestled in soft, protective material. Two matching pairs. Mine, obviously much smaller. But Jorik's? They were big enough to wrap around my calves, the carving so complex and detailed I knew I could stare at them for hours. The cuffs were a mix of tones—platinum, pewter, silver and gold—all woven together into an alien design that played tricks on the eyes.

Wulf lifted the larger cuffs, stood and held them out for me.

"No one's going to miss seeing these on him," I said, taking the larger pair from him. They were heavy, solid. Wide. Very permanent. I looked up, way up, at Wulf. "Thank you."

"You are welcome. I will find Jorik and ensure he goes to your quarters immediately."

I sighed, trying to calm my racing heart. "This may be harder to do, but would you watch Jori for us while we... while we, you know." I blushed, even though Wulf knew what we were going to do. Mating cuffs meant one thing. Claiming. And that meant wild beast sex. "I fed him not too long ago. And with Jorik parading him around earlier, he'll probably sleep most of the time."

His eyes widened in surprise and then he smiled brilliantly. He was so handsome. Not as hot as Jorik, but still. Atlan.

Apparently, I had a *thing* for beast men. He was going to make some female *very* happy. I just had to hope it would be soon.

He quickly frowned. "I will do as you request and send him to you, but he won't let go of that baby for anything."

I looked up at him slyly. "Tell him his mate is naked and waiting for him."

He looked away from me at that. "His beast will rip me to pieces just mentioning you are naked."

I laughed, because the possibility was true. "You want to hold that baby, I'm sure you'll come up with something."

I walked off then, knowing Wulf was determined to babysit. Jorik had refused to let Jori out of his sight since the fiasco with Wendy, despite the fact that Kai had done as he'd promised and kept Jori safe and protected.

We split up, Wulf headed to find Jorik, I to our quarters. We both had a mission and neither of us would be defeated.

~

Jorik

I STORMED INTO OUR QUARTERS, a mixture of angry, frustrated and aroused.

"Mate!" I bellowed. She was not in the main room, but the sight of her had me pausing in the doorway to the bedroom. "Fuck," I murmured.

There was Gabriela, *my* Gabriela, lying on her side, her elbow bent and her head propped up on her hand. Naked. One leg was angled and tipped over the other, hiding her sweet pussy from sight. Her arm was across her breasts and covered her nipples, but their lush size couldn't be concealed.

She was a vision. *Mine.* Gorgeous. *Mine.* A temptress. *Mine.*

"Gabriela," I murmured. *Mine.*

My beast kept repeating that one word over and over as my cock hardened impossibly more.

It was only when she picked up the cuffs and let them dangle from her fingers that I noticed them. Mating cuffs. The cuffs I had ordered for her from Atlan.

"You are mine, Jorik," she said.

I nodded. "Yes."

"I will not have other females trying to take you away from me. Therefore, I am putting mating cuffs on you and claiming you as my own."

I arched a brow. Grinned. Only Gabriela would do things so differently.

No, this wasn't different. This was *our* normal.

"Yes, mate," I said. "How did you get them?" She didn't say anything. "Ah, let me guess. Wulf?"

She shrugged.

"The cuffs aren't the only part of the claiming," I advised.

"Wulf said as much."

I frowned, took a step into the room. "Do not speak of another male while you are naked and in our bed, mate."

She looked up at me through her lashes.

"Wulf also said—"

"Mate," I warned.

"—the same thing, that the cuffs weren't the only part of an Atlan claiming. I told him you'd take care of the rest."

Fuck.

"That's right," I growled. I reached up, tugged off my shirt, then stripped completely at a record pace. "My beast and I know just how to fuck you to make you ours permanently. It's going to be rough, Gabriela."

"Okay," she whispered, and I watched her squirm.

"I'm going to take you hard. Deep."

"Jorik."

"Up against the wall, your arms pinned."

She sat up and reached for me. "Now, Jorik."

Yes. Now.

She took one of the larger cuffs and held it out. I gave her my wrist and watched as she placed the symbol of our mating on my arm, clicked it into place.

Glancing up at me, she said, "You. Are.

Mine. Jorik. We might not have been matched by a stupid computer, but we're perfect for each other." She picked up the second cuff, wrapped it around my other wrist.

My beast howled with happiness as I felt the cool heaviness of the cuffs. I reveled in the permanence of them. I would wear them with pride, so everyone knew I belonged to Gabriela, that I was hers. Completely.

And her love saved me from ever worrying about losing control, going into Mating Fever, becoming more beast than male. The cuffs ensured my complete surrender to her, to loving her, belonging to her, protecting her and our children with my life.

My beast settled, content in a way that shocked me, even as he stirred with hunger... for her.

Reaching down, I grabbed the cuffs from the bed for her wrists. As I put them on her, I said, "Mine. No one else's. One look and I knew you belonged to me.

Never will you be taken from me again. Never will we be apart. You are mine and I am yours."

When finished, when the elaborate cuffs were about her wrists, she leapt into my arms and kissed me. The feel of her soft skin, her breasts pressed into my chest and her ass when I cupped it, held her against me... heaven.

Her legs circled about my waist and my cock was between us, hard, thick and insistent. Turning, I kissed and walked toward the nearest wall, carefully pressed her against it so there was no way she was getting away. She would feel every hard inch of me, know my power, my control.

I felt the heft of the cuffs on my own wrists and knew this was everything. This intimate ritual filled me with primitive needs. Gabriela wanted it. My beast craved it. And I did, too. The connection, the permanent bonding of us made my need for her so intense. I wanted to claim, possess, fill her body as well as her heart.

After the complete nightmare that had

been Warden Morda, I was more sure than ever. More adamant. In a rush. A pounding need to finish this made my cock throb, my hold fervent.

"Jorik," she breathed as I licked and nipped my way down her neck. With one hand cupping her ass, the other holding her wrists above her head, she was at my mercy.

I worked my way lower, over her collarbone and down to the swell of her breast, kissing and circling until I eventually laved her nipple. I was gentle, for I knew Jori's nursing had made them sensitive. One, then the other, got my attention before I kissed her again, her tongue finding mine.

I couldn't hold back any longer. I throbbed, ached to fill her. My balls were pulled up tight, ready to fill her with my seed. I knew it would not take since she'd been given a shot by the doctor, but the instinctive need to breed her would never go away. When she was ready for another child, I would give it to her.

Pulling back, I shifted enough so my cock settled at her entrance.

"Mate, look at me," I growled.

Her dark gaze fluttered open, met mine.

"I claim you. Now. Forever."

"Yes."

That was all I had to hear, all my beast wanted and I plunged deep, pulling her down onto me.

She cried out, her inner walls clenching and squeezing me. Fuck, I wasn't going to last. Her wet heat engulfed me.

"I claim you, too, Jorik. Now. Forever. Now fuck me. Hard."

Yes, my little warrior. She'd punched Wendy Morda with the strength of an Atlan beast, but I knew it was her mother's fury. No one fucked with my child. And knowing Gabriela was such a fierce protector made my beast proud, my heart overflow.

I pulled back, thrust hard, just as she wanted. "Yes, mate."

I let my beast take control, grow in size, lifting her with me as I grew taller. My cock grew inside her, and she leaned her head back, bit her lip in a way I'd come to need to see. She moaned as my cock grew. My beast had been there the entire time, holding back, waiting for his turn.

Now he was starved for her, for this final claiming.

"Mine." His growl was nearly a roar, and she whispered my name, over and over, as I pulled in and out of her wet heat, thrust deep. Made her mine forever.

My fingers stroked along the cuffs on her wrists as I held her in place. She wasn't going anywhere, completely filled with my cock. Her heels dug into my ass, urging me on. I took her, fast. Rough. Wild. The sound of flesh slapping to-gether mixed with our ragged breathing. Our skin became slick with sweat. We were desperate, frantic.

She felt so incredibly good, I didn't want to leave her body. Ever. My pleasure was right there before me, but I would have her come first. Reaching between us, I found her clit, brushed it gently with my finger.

Her eyes widened and held mine. "Come," my beast ordered. "Now." He would not take no for an answer, and I carefully pinched her clit.

That did it. My mate liked it a little rough, a whole lot wild. Her inner walls rippled and pulled me deeper inside her body as she cried out her pleasure. I fucked her through it, but I was only so strong. My beast submitted to her in that moment, giving her everything. My body, my seed, my heart.

I roared my release, emptying into her.

I knew. We were matched. Claimed. She was mine. We didn't need the cuffs to keep us close.

I turned, walked over to the bed, still buried deep as I pushed my beast back. I wanted her, too. She was mine, and I wanted her in bed, her softness surrounding me. I lowered us carefully to the mattress, settling her on top of me. I wouldn't pull out, but would stay in her until she was ready to go again. I was still hard; I didn't think that would change anytime soon.

"When we are recovered, I will taste you, mate. Every inch," I said, stroking her sweaty back.

"I'm not an ice cream cone," she countered, her head resting on my chest.

I smiled, remembering her behind the counter at the store on Earth, offering me a delicious treat each time I saw her. "No, but you're my favorite flavor."

I flipped us, so she was pinned beneath me. I began kissing her, licking her skin, tasting her. Her unique flavor. I would never get enough.

"I love you, Gabriela. Every cell in my body loves you."

Her pussy clamped, rippled around me with the words. "Jorik."

I thrust. She moaned, her arms settling in my hair. She pulled my face to hers and kissed me. Gently.

"I love you, too. You're mine now. Beast and all."

Especially my beast, but I didn't need to tell her that. He had all night to *show* her.

16

G abriela, Three Days Later

"HE IS NOT a toy to be played with," Jorik grumbled. He held Jori in a snug football hold against his chest and had no intention of giving him up. The glint of his mating cuff reminded me again he was mine, that this was truly everything I ever wanted.

Jorik was mine and would always be.

Wendy was long gone, transported to

Prillon Prime, escorted by two Everian Hunters. Warden Egara had assured all of us that Jorik's testing had been erased from the system entirely, ensuring there was no chance of that fiasco happening again.

I smiled at Jorik, but when he glared at me, I tried to stifle it. It wasn't working.

"Wulf got to babysit him when you claimed me—"

"I claimed you quite well," he said, leaning down to murmur it.

I couldn't help but blush. "Quite well," I confirmed. "But everyone wants a turn."

"At claiming you?" he teased.

"At babysitting."

"If we let everyone have a turn babysitting, we will not see Jori again until he is twelve."

I rolled my eyes. "That is not true," I countered.

We entered the cafeteria where many of those on The Colony were waiting. They clapped and stood for us and Jorik wrapped his free arm about my shoulders, his chest going nearly beast size with pride. At first, I hadn't really understood the mating cuffs. On Earth, a wedding ring—for a lot of women—was a sign that she was loved by someone. Claimed by a *man.* Wanted. Desired. An outward sign of "hands off." There was a lot of messed up psychology in that, and I'd tried to make sense of it.

But here? It was the opposite. Those cuffs meant *he* was worthy of being claimed, mated, *chosen.* The juxtaposition struck me as odd—alien—but I couldn't disagree with how it made me feel, and I wondered if a man on Earth felt the same way I was feeling now, when he put an engagement ring on the finger of the woman he loved.

He was *MINE.* M. I. N. E. And now, everyone on this planet, and every other planet, would know it. Even Wendy.

I was territorial. That was it. I'd turned into a territorial, primitive she-beast.

And I didn't care. Then again, I'd been put in a transport box and almost sent to

God knew where. I had a right to pee on Jorik's leg if I wanted.

Based on the dreadfully high number of unmated males on The Colony, it wasn't often someone found their mate. Our story was definitely unique and full of challenges. But we were together now, and I had my beast cuffed.

I should have been shocked when Jorik told me he couldn't take them off—wouldn't take them off—until his death. Instead I felt... content. Forever meant forever, and that was just fine with me.

"I am so happy for you!" Rachel said, coming up to us, hugging me. "And mad. I told you to call me if you needed someone to watch Jori. You had *two* people babysit."

"Special circumstances," I replied. "Besides, you have Max."

Her little boy was in her arms. At almost two years old, he seemed so big in comparison to Jori. He looked just like his father, Maxim, with his copper colored skin and dark hair. The way Rachel was looking at Jori, I was pretty sure she'd have a new one of her own soon enough. Maybe a girl, who would be golden like Ryston, her other mate.

The boy wriggled in her hold and she set him down. The toddler ran off toward his fathers. "Yes, but there's nothing like that newborn smell."

"Everyone line up and you may each have a turn holding Jori," Jorik announced.

I looked up at him, smiled.

He was so serious, so stern looking. Not a kind, gentle father but a protector. Well, both, but his inner beast was guarding the baby fiercely.

"Let's go sit down," I told him, pointing to some open chairs.

Reluctantly, he sat down and kept Jori tucked in close. The baby was awake now and looking out at everyone.

Max ran up to Jorik and stood directly between his parted knees. He pointed a chubby finger. "Baby."

Maxim—I had to struggle to think of him as anything other than the governor

—came over and scooped him up, dangling him upside down by his ankles. "You're my baby," he said, swinging him back and forth like a metronome. The boy squealed, his laughter making everyone smile.

"All right, let me hold him," Rachel said, bold enough—or perhaps eager enough—to face Jorik first.

"Let her hold him," I whispered.

"Has she washed her hands?" he asked, eying her with doubt.

She huffed and held her hands out and Jorik relented. Rachel took our son and snuggled him close, leaned down and breathed him in. I knew that feeling, that smell, that sweet snuggle only a newborn had. She turned and walked off with Jori.

"Where the hell is she going?" Jorik snapped, trying to stand. I tugged on his wrist, kept him down.

"Let him go."

"Next you'll be telling me he can take one of the shuttles out."

I laughed, realizing a father was a father, no matter what planet. "I think he needs to be able to sit up first."

Wulf came over to us, blocking Jorik's view of everyone. Jorik shoved at his hip. "Get out of my way. If I can't hold Jori, I need to be able to see him."

Wulf shifted to his left, giving Jorik a clear view.

"Congratulations." Wulf tipped his chin toward us, and I held up my cuffs. I hadn't believed they would ensure we remained close, making it painful for Jorik and I to be physically parted by too much distance. I'd tested it, having Jorik sit on the side of the bed as I left the quarters. I'd made it partway down the hall when it hurt. Holy hell, the pain, the feeling of horrible separation had swamped me. I'd run back to the room and jumped Jorik.

He'd assured me that I could remove the cuffs any time I needed to, but that he would not. An Atlan, he said, prided himself on enduring the pain of that separation. It was, in his words, a reminder of the gift he'd been given in claiming a female and kept those riding the edge of Mating Fever from losing control of their beasts.

Men. Males. Whatever. I had not enjoyed the strong zap of pain our separation had caused. If he had to go out on a mission, I would have to take the cuffs off.

I almost looked forward to it, knowing just how badly Jorik would want to place them on my wrists again. Naked.

Wyatt ran by. He was wearing a cape about his neck and had a child's size Coalition belt about his waist. On it was a fake ion pistol and a few other items most fighters carried. I'd heard from Rachel and Wulf that Lindsey's mother had joined her and Wyatt from Earth.

Her mother, Carla, was smiling now, speaking to one of the older Prillon males in the far corner of the room. Or should I say, he was leaning in, standing *very* close.

Did he just sniff her hair?

I placed my hand on Jorik's arm, about to ask.

If I didn't know better...

"He's so adorable, right?" I asked, pointing at the child.

"Wyatt? Yes. Fine boy, but I think Jori will be bigger. Stronger."

I had no doubt of that.

"Are there any many little girls here?" I wondered. There was more than enough testosterone, that was for sure.

"Tia Zakar. Her fathers are Hunt and Tyran."

"Prillons?" I wondered about them. I'd heard of Kristin, the other human female here who, like Rachel, was mated to two Prillon warriors, but I had yet to see her. "Kristin, right? From Earth?"

"Yes. But she has been hunting in the caverns of Base 5 for a few days. Her mates accompanied her. Of course, they took the child."

"Into caverns?"

Of course they did. I grinned, eager to meet another human woman, and especially one sassy enough to drag two Prillon mates with her so she could go *hunting* for Hive in underground caves.

She sounded like some kind of super woman.

"There are also Rezzer's twins. One is a girl." Jorik looked about. It seemed like he was searching for these twins, but I knew he was watching Jori, who'd been taken from Rachel and was now being held by a Prillon who was more cyborg than anything else. But, he was smiling down at Jori and his hold was so gentle.

Speak of the devils. Two smaller toddlers screamed and ran by. The little girl was running after her brother. While she wore pink and had bows in her hair, she was fast and the way she tackled her brother into a fierce hug and kissed his cheek, was not going to be timid.

Rezzer, a giant beast, scooped the little girl up and carried her over to us.

"You need to make one of these," he said, smiling down at his daughter. She had similar coloring and patted his cheek. "An older boy is good, but then you must have a girl. You think you're protective of your son, Jorik? Just wait."

He kissed the little girl's head and then set her in Jorik's lap. She popped up and stood on his thighs, then patted Jorik's cheeks. His eyes widened and he grinned, holding her little waist so she didn't fall.

"Mate, I want a little girl," he said, looking at CJ as he spoke to me.

Yes, a girl as sweet as little CJ, but with Jorik's looks... my ovaries were ready.

"She must look just like you," he said, turning to stare at me, the heat in his eyes one I never could have imagined before I met him. Adoration. Love. Total and complete acceptance.

My heart flipped and I smiled.

"All right."

His eyes widened and he stared. "All right? Now?"

I'd had the birth control shot from the medical unit, but I knew it was reversible. "I'll go to the doctor so we can start once it's worn off. But until then, we can... practice."

In an instant, Jorik was on his feet,

little CJ dangling in the air as he held her out in front of him. He walked over to her father, handed her off.

Jorik looked for Jori, saw he was in another Atlan's arms, sound asleep. "Kai!"

The alien looked to Jorik.

"Watch Jori."

"It is my honor." Kai's smile was huge, and I realized he'd been worried that Jorik—or I—would blame him for what happened with Wendy. The crazy woman. I would stop thinking her name and just refer to her as that, *the crazy woman.*

Jorik took my hand and tugged me toward the door.

"Wait! I thought I got to babysit!" Rachel called.

Jorik turned, faced her. "You all must keep him alive and happy or you will deal with my beast. Now, I must deal with my mate."

Before I could gasp in utter shock at his boldness, Jorik leaned down and tossed me over his shoulder. When I wiggled, he slapped my ass and carried me from the cafeteria and down the hall.

"You want to practice, mate, for a little girl? I'll give you practice. And later, we will reverse that shot and make one for real."

I wasn't going to argue with my mate on this. As I watched the play of his taut ass as he walked us to our quarters, I knew life couldn't be any better. Although, if Jorik had his way, soon, we would have a little girl.

Perfect.

A SPECIAL THANK YOU TO MY READERS...

Want more? I've got **hidden** bonus content on my web site **exclusively** for those on my mailing list.

If you are already on my email list, you don't need to do a thing! Simply scroll to the bottom of my newsletter emails and click on the **super-secret** link.

Not a member? What are you waiting for? In addition to ALL of my bonus content (great new stuff will be added regularly) you will be the first to hear about my newest release the second it hits the stores—AND you will get a free book as a special welcome gift.

Sign up now! http://freescifiromance.com

FIND YOUR INTERSTELLAR MATCH!

YOUR mate is out there. Take the test today and discover your perfect match. Are you ready for a sexy alien mate (or two)?

VOLUNTEER NOW!

interstellarbridesprogram.com

DO YOU LOVE AUDIOBOOKS?

Grace Goodwin's books are now available as audiobooks...everywhere.

LET'S TALK SPOILER ROOM!

Interested in joining my **Sci-Fi Squad**? Meet new like-minded sci-fi romance fanatics and chat with Grace! Get excerpts, cover reveals and sneak peeks before anyone else. Be part of a private Facebook group that shares pictures and fun news! Join here:

https://www.facebook.com/groups/scifisquad/

***

Want to talk about Grace Goodwin books with others? Join the **SPOILER ROOM** and spoil away! Your GG BFFs are waiting! (And so is Grace)

Join here:

https://www.facebook.com/
groups/ggspoilerroom/

GET A FREE BOOK!

Join my mailing list to be the first to know of new releases, free books, special prices and other author giveaways.

http://freescifiromance.com

ALSO BY GRACE GOODWIN

Interstellar Brides® Program

Mastered by Her Mates

Assigned a Mate

Mated to the Warriors

Claimed by Her Mates

Taken by Her Mates

Mated to the Beast

Tamed by the Beast

Mated to the Vikens

Her Mate's Secret Baby

Mating Fever

Her Viken Mates

Fighting For Their Mate

Her Rogue Mates

Claimed By The Vikens

The Commanders' Mate

Matched and Mated

Hunted

Viken Command

Trinity: Ascension Saga - Volume 1

Ascension Saga, book 4

Ascension Saga, book 5

Ascension Saga, book 6

Faith: Ascension Saga - Volume 2

Ascension Saga, book 7

Ascension Saga, book 8

Ascension Saga, book 9

Destiny: Ascension Saga - Volume 3

Other Books

Their Conquered Bride

Wild Wolf Claiming: A Howl's Romance

ABOUT GRACE

Grace Goodwin is a *USA Today* and international bestselling author of Sci-Fi & Paranormal romance. Grace believes all women should be treated like royalty, in the bedroom and out of it, and writes love stories where men know how to make their women feel pampered, protected and very well taken care of. Grace hates the snow, loves the mountains (yes, that's a problem) and wishes she could simply download the stories out of her head instead of being forced to type them out. Grace lives in the western US and is a full-time writer, an avid reader and an admitted caffeine addict. She is active on Facebook and loves to chat with readers and fellow sci-fi fanatics.

All of Grace's books can be read as

sexy, stand-alone adventures. But be careful, she likes her heroes hot and her love scenes hotter. You have been warned...

www.gracegoodwin.com
gracegoodwinauthor@gmail.com

CYBORG'S
SECRET BABY

INTERSTELLAR BRIDES® PROGRAM: THE
COLONY - 7

GRACE GOODWIN

GET A FREE BOOK!

JOIN MY MAILING LIST TO BE THE FIRST TO KNOW OF NEW RELEASES, FREE BOOKS, SPECIAL PRICES AND OTHER AUTHOR GIVEAWAYS.

http://freescifiromance.com